the Cheetah girls

Dorinda's Secret

Deborah Gregory

JUMP AT THE SUN

HYPERION PAPERBACKS FOR CHILDREN

NEW YORK

Fashion credits: Photography by Charlie Pizzarello. Models: Sabrina Millen, Sonya Millen, Imani Parks, and Brandi Stewart. On Imani (Dorinda): Jacket and gloves by P. Fields. Dresses by Betsey Johnson. Tops by Nicole Miller, XOXO, and Dollhouse. Pants by XOXO. Jackets by Trash and Vaudeville. Shoes by Nicole Miller. Stockings by Sox Trot. Hair Accessories by Head Dress. Hair by Julie McIntosh. Makeup by Lanier Long and Deborah Wallace. Fashion styling by Nole Marin.

Printed in the United States of America
First Edition
1 3 5 7 9 10 8 6 4 2
This book is set in 12-point Palatino.
ISBN: 0-7868-1426-8
Library of Congress Catalog Card Number: 99-67726.
Visit www.cheetahgirls.com

For Abiola, who runs for her breakfast
before she says *"Hola!"*
to the mouse in the house
who peeps her granola!

The Cheetah Girls Credo

To earn my spots and rightful place in the world, I solemnly swear to honor and uphold the Cheetah Girls oath:

☙ Cheetah Girls don't litter, they glitter. I will help my family, friends, and other Cheetah Girls whenever they need my love, support, or a *really* big hug.

☙ All Cheetah Girls are created equal, but we are not alike. We come in different sizes, shapes, and colors, and hail from different cultures. I will not judge others by the color of their spots, but by their character.

A true Cheetah Girl doesn't spend more time doing her hair than her homework. Hair extensions may be career extensions, but talent and skills will pay my bills.

 True Cheetah Girls *can* achieve without a weave—or a wiggle, jiggle, or a giggle. I promise to rely (mostly) on my brains, heart, and courage to reach my cheetah-licious potential!

 A brave Cheetah Girl isn't afraid to admit when she's scared. I promise to get on my knees and summon the growl power of the Cheetah Girls who came before me—including my mom, grandmoms, and the Supremes— and ask them to help me be strong.

 All Cheetah Girls make mistakes. I promise to admit when I'm wrong and will work to make it right. I'll also say I'm sorry, even when I don't want to.

 Grown-ups are not always right, but they are bigger, older, and louder. I will treat my teachers, parents, and people of authority with respect—and expect them to do the same!

- True Cheetah Girls don't run with wolves or hang with hyenas. True Cheetahs pick much better friends. I will not try to get other people's approval by acting like a copycat.

- To become the Cheetah Girl that only *I* can be, I promise not to follow anyone else's dreams but my own. No matter how much I quiver, shake, shiver, and quake!

- Cheetah Girls were born for adventure. I promise to learn a language other than my own and travel around the world to meet my fellow Cheetah Girls.

Chapter 1

When I see my foster mother, Mrs. Bosco, sprawled out on the bed in her teeny cubbyhole of a bedroom, I know right away that something is up. I immediately get this squiggly spasm in my stomach. She never lies down in there before bedtime unless she's upset or sick. Either way, it's bad news.

I know she had to go down to the agency today—the Administration of Children's Services in Brooklyn—which is supposedly responsible for the lives of thousands of foster kids like me in the Big Apple. This can only mean one thing, I figure—we've lost custody of Corky!

"Please don't tell me they are going to take

Corky away!" I pray. "If anybody has to go, let it be Kenya."

Now I know that's a terrible thing to say, but you've got to understand—my foster sister Kenya is spastic-on-the-elastic tip. She's only six, and I don't want to be around when she's old enough to *really* start ad-lipping—running her mouth off the cuff, if you know what I'm saying.

Before you think we've got it on easy street or something, let me tell you about the other foster kids living here with Mr. and Mrs. Bosco. Besides myself—Dorinda Rogers (or Do' Re Mi, as my crew, the Cheetah Girls, call me)—there are five other girls. Kenya shares a room with five-year-old Arba (from Albania—she's the newest member of our foster family) and my favorite sister, Twinkie. I share my bedroom with Chantelle (who hogs *my* computer) and Monie the Meanie (who spends most of her time with her boyfriend these days).

But wait—I'm not done yet! There are also five boys! There's Corky, who I've already mentioned. Then there's Khalil, Nestor, precious Topwe (his mother is from Africa!), and last but not least, Shawn the Fawn.

So, as you can see, Mr. and Mrs. Bosco really have their hands full. The Boscos aren't getting any younger, either—they're old enough to be grandparents—and Mrs. Bosco's been sick on and off, the past couple of years. So the last thing they need is trouble with family court.

Which brings me back to Corky. He has lived with us since he was crawling around in diapers and eating lint off the floor. Four years later, his father comes out of the blue, trying to win back custody. Where was "Daddykins" back then, huh?

Now Mrs. Bosco has to bring Corky all the way to Brooklyn for monthly visits with "Mister Good-for-Nothing"—that's what she calls Corky's father, Mr. Dorgle. Mrs. Bosco even has to go to family court for the custody proceedings.

"I wish a judge would just hit that fool over the head with a gavel and be done with it. Case closed," Mrs. Bosco says, turning on her other side to face me.

"I know that's right," I humph nervously, because I just dread what's coming. I feel stupid hovering in the doorway, but Mrs. Bosco's bedroom is really tiny, so I never go in there unless she says I can.

"Come on and sit on the bed, Dorinda," Mrs. Bosco says, chuckling and wheezing at the same time. I sit on the edge of the bed, trying not to take up any space.

"I spent the whole day fighting with those people," Mrs. Bosco says, putting her hand on her forehead like it hurts.

"Those people" are what she calls the case-workers, who "push a lot of paper around doing nothing."

"I swear they got on my last nerve today," she continues, her Southern drawl more pro-nounced than usual because she's upset. She raises herself up from the bed, then puts on her glasses and squints at me. "Dorinda, how come your eyes are red?"

"I guess I was rubbing them because I'm tired," I say, yawning. "You know I had dance class tonight at the Y."

"Oh, yeah, how is that Truly child?" Mrs. Bosco asks, chuckling softly.

"Still teaching us more combinations than Bugga Bear Jones does in the ring," I chuckle back. Bugga Bear Jones is Mr. Bosco's favorite boxer. Mr. Bosco watches boxing on the television at his night job as a security guard. "That Truly child" would be my dance teacher, Darlene Truly, who is, well, "truly" dope.

Mrs. Bosco calls everybody "child," because sometimes she can't remember their names. I can tell by the way she chuckles that she likes Ms. Truly, though. After all, Ms. Truly did hook me up with an audition as a backup dancer for one of the dopest dope singers on the planet— Mo' Money Monique. I got the job, too, but in the end I didn't take it—partly because of Mrs. Bosco, and partly because of my crew, the Cheetah Girls.

Yeah, the Cheetah Girls are in the house. Besides me, that would be Galleria "Bubbles" Garibaldi; Chanel "Chuchie" Simmons; and the hot-sauce twins from Houston, Texas, Aquanette and Anginette Walker. (Every week we have new nicknames for the twins—but to their faces, we call them Aqua and Angie for short.)

We're not just a crew, either. We're a supachili singing group. I'm not just flossin'—we're waiting to hear from Def Duck records, 'cuz they're talkin' about us making a demo, and then maybe even a record deal!

That was after I turned down the Mo' Money Monique job, though. I didn't turn it down because I knew the Cheetah Girls were about to hit it big—I did it because I love my crew. I love my foster family, too—even Kenya. I was just riffing about her before 'cuz she gets on my nerves. Nope—no way was I gonna leave my crew or my foster family—because they're really all I have.

"Do you know that fool had the nerve not to show up today?" Mrs. Bosco says, shaking her head. "He should just leave this child alone and hide back under whatever rock he crawled out of." I can tell Mrs. Bosco is just getting started. "Where I come from, he woulda never seen the inside of no courtroom. We woulda just chased him out of town with a shotgun nipping at his heels, and dared that fool to look back!"

Mrs. Bosco was "born and raised in good ole Henderson, NC," as she likes to say. NC—that's North Carolina. She is very old, and she comes from a long line of tobacco sharecroppers. She had to work in the fields when she was only eight years old, and she never went to school. That's why Mrs. Bosco is illiterate—even though we're not supposed to know that, and certainly the social workers aren't! They wouldn't let us live here if they knew, and then where would all of us be?

You know, Mrs. Bosco's being illiterate really cost me, too. She wanted to adopt me, but she didn't understand the procedure, so the adoption never went through. She and Mr. Bosco threw me a big party before we found out. She says she's still going to adopt me, but I don't ask her about it anymore.

"I'm tired of them fooling with Corky's mind," she goes on. "How can they even consider putting him with Mr. Good-for-Nothing is beyond me, but that's typical, you know."

I breathe a sigh of relief, now that I know it's just another round in the custody battle, and nothing final has been decided.

"Even after him not showing up, they are still gonna continue with this mess," Mrs. Bosco adds, taking off her glasses and lying back down on her bed. "Oh, by the way, Dorinda—*your* caseworker is coming by here tomorrow to see y'all. What's her name again?"

"Mrs. Tattle," I say, reminding her. "I'll come

straight home after vocal class. How come she's coming on a Saturday?"

"She said she had to see you—that probably just means she's leaving for her vacation and needs to finish up her paperwork," Mrs. Bosco says with a sigh.

Mrs. Bosco is probably right. I've had more caseworkers than I can count—sometimes I can't even remember their names, because they come and go so fast. Some of them look kinda sad—like they wish they were someplace else, doing something different.

I know what that's like. Before I started school at Fashion Industries East High—where I met my crew and became a Cheetah Girl—I didn't have many *real* friends, and I wasn't sure what I was going to do with my life. Now I know: I'm going to sing, dance, make costumes—and make people happy, too.

Kenya lets out a scream loud enough to chase my daydreams away. I look back at Mrs. Bosco, but she is nodding off again, so I whisper, "I'll see you later." She does that all the time. She can be talking one minute, then sleeping the next. Like a cat, I guess.

Walking toward the kitchen, I call out, "What

are y'all doing in there?" As usual, *someone* is trying to get at some food in the kitchen cupboard. "You know you're not supposed to be climbing on the counter, Kenya. How many times does Mrs. Bosco have to tell you that?" I shake my head. Kenya never listens to anybody.

"I want some popcorn!" she yells.

"I'll get it," I tell her, then pull up a chair and stand on it to reach the big bag of Brand Ann popcorn. Like I said before, Kenya is always whining about something and never shares anything with the rest of us. I know she steals candy and stuff from stores, because sometimes I find the wrappers under her bed or they fall out of her backpack and pockets. When I do, she just gives me this blank look, like she doesn't know how they got there.

When I first came to live at Mrs. Bosco's, I was really angry—I guess because my mother abandoned me, and then my first foster mother gave me up. I used to steal candy, too, but I stopped doing it after a while, when I wasn't so mad anymore. Maybe Kenya will settle down someday, too. I sure hope so.

Peering into the oven, I see my plate of food,

covered in tin foil. The kids have all eaten dinner, and as usual, Mrs. Bosco has left me something for when I get home from class—but I'm too tired to look and see what it is. I just take the bag of popcorn into the living room and plop down in front of the television.

I give Corky the first handful, even though that makes Kenya mad. "Thank you," he says, his pretty greenish-gray eyes sparkling at me. He is so cute—I can't understand why anyone would give him away, even though I know everything is not so simple as that. Grown-ups have lots of problems, and sometimes they just can't deal with them.

I pass around handfuls of popcorn to Khalil, Arba, Twinkie, Topwe, and Shawn, who are all sitting around waiting for their favorite show to come on TV.

Corky puts his hand out for more. "I'm gonna call you Porky instead of Corky," I chuckle, watching his mischievous grin get bigger. Corky's mother was put away in a "mental health facility." I know this because I help with the paperwork and bills, so I can't help reading some of the files and reports we get.

I'll bet you if Corky's mother could see how

cute he is now, it would make her mental illness go away. Sometimes people aren't really crazy, Mrs. Bosco says—they're just tired and confused. Maybe Corky's mother is like that.

"Stop pushing me!" Kenya screams at Nestor, who is trying to get a better seat in front of the television. Nestor just ignores Kenya. He is eight, and kinda quiet. Sometimes he sits at the table and eats so fast he never even looks up at anybody. That's how he got his nickname, "Nestlé's Quik." As usual, he has already gobbled his handful of popcorn—earning his nickname to the max.

Zoning out in front of the television, I just munch away, staring at the stupid commercials.

"Gimme more!" my brother Topwe moans. I just hand him the bag of popcorn, because I'm so tired of him trying to take it on the sneak tip. Brand Ann tastes like a whole bunch of air anyway—it's not the good stuff, like Piggly Wiggly Chedda Puffs, which sticks to your fingers and has a supa-cheesy flow.

"You ate it *olle*, Dori-i-n-da!" Topwe says, peering up at me and baring the mile-wide gap between his two front teeth. Topwe cracks me up, because he speaks English with his own African groove. Topwe was born HIV-positive because his mother was a crack addict. Sometimes he comes down with nasty colds, but basically he's okay—and he eats "like a hungry hog." That's what the twins, Aqua and Angie, said after they saw Topwe in action at my "adoption" party.

Aqua and Angie made the bomb spread of yum-yums for everyone to eat, but Topwe ate the whole tray of candied yams before anybody else got a whiff of it. His name means vegetable in some African dialect, so I guess the yams were a good choice, you know what I'm saying? Now Topwe keeps asking me when the twins are coming back over with some more "kaandied yoms."

"I want some more!" Kenya moans, poking out her mouth in a pout.

"Mom, can we open the other bag of popcorn?" I call out to Mrs. Bosco. Ever since I almost got adopted, she said it was okay to call her "Mom," so I do. I mean, I've lived here seven years, so I don't think she's gonna give me away.

"Just make sure the kids don't leave kernels

all over the floor," Mrs. Bosco yells back.

"Okay—um," I say, holding back on calling her Mom again. I don't want to overdo it or anything.

"When is this over?" Kenya asks when the news brief comes on after the commercial.

"Soon, just watch," I reply. I'm so tired I would watch anything. Of course, they're all waiting for their favorite show to come on— *She's All That and a Pussy Cat.*

"Oh, it's the news," whines Khalil. "I hate the news. It always makes me sad."

The news announcer says, "Now, more on Paulo Rivera's Fib-ulous Ride." A picture of a cute boy flashes on the television screen. The reporter continues, "A thirteen-year-old boy's tall tale of his solo odyssey from the Dominican Republic to New York in search of his only living relative turns out to be a journey in his imagination."

Now my eyes are glued to the television screen. Even Kenya stops fidgeting as the reporter talks about this boy, Paulo Rivera, who ran away from home and took a bus from New Jersey to the Big Apple. Apparently he told everyone that he had run away from Santo

Domingo in the Dominican Republic and traveled 2,000 miles on his own—all the way to New York!

"Paulo claimed he was searching for his father," says the reporter. "But the father, it turns out, died of AIDS a year ago. 'Paulo attended the funeral, but still refuses to believe it,' says the boy's tearful aunt, with whom Paulo lived in New Jersey. The aunt reported him missing when he didn't come home from school.

"It's not clear what will happen to Paulo Rivera, who is now under the care of the Administration for Children's Services. ACS officials could not be reached for comment," the reporter says, finishing the news report.

Suddenly, I feel sorry for Paulo. All that trouble he went through, just to end up in foster care. It doesn't seem fair.

"That's cold he got caught," says Khalil, who is glued to the television screen. He has only lived at Mrs. Bosco's for a few months and has been in a lot of foster homes. He kinda keeps to himself, even though he's cool. "If that had been me, I would have been Audi 5000—they would have never found me, yo."

"How come?" I ask—because I'm really curious how an eleven-year-old kid thinks he could disappear and live by himself.

"'Cuz when I ran away from my last foster home, they didn't find me. I came back by myself," Khalil says, like *he's* bragging or something.

"How many foster homes wuz you in?" Nestor asks.

"Four," Khalil says, like he's talking about trophies.

"I was in three," Nestor says, like *he's* bragging.

"I almost got adopted," Chantelle blurts out.

Hmmm. I've never heard this one before. Maybe Chantelle is fibbing, just to get attention.

"No you didn't," Nestor says nastily.

"Yes I did, but I didn't want to stay," Chantelle says.

Twinkie nuzzles up to me and puts her head on my shoulder, her fuzzy hair flouncing all the over the place. "I bet you that boy *wuz* looking for *somebody*."

Twinkie is so smart. "Yeah. I bet you he was," I reply, then hold her tight while we watch the show.

"I wanna find my father," Khalil announces.

It's the first time he's ever said anything like that. I notice that Nestor is pretending he's not listening.

"How do you know you've got a father?" Chantelle asks, with an attitude.

"'Cuz I do. My mother told me," Khalil says matter-of-factly.

"You have a mother?" I ask, surprised.

"Of course I have a mother, stupid," Khalil says, getting annoyed now.

"Well, *I* don't," I say, just to show him I'm not stupid.

"Yes you do," Khalil says. "Everybody has a mother."

"Well, I never *saw* her!" I exclaim, embarrassed.

"Don't you ever want to find your mother?" Nestor asks, ganging up on me too.

"I don't know," I say, determined not to let them win. I'm not going to tell them about my sister at Mrs. Parkay's—she was my first foster mother, the one who gave me away. I try not to think about her anymore, because Mrs. Parkay probably doesn't want to see me anymore—and I sure don't want to see her.

"I'll bet you *my* mother has long hair like an

angel," Twinkie says, smiling. "I know she's gonna come and get me one day."

I can't believe Twinkie said that! When I was younger, I used to think the same thing. Of course, I don't anymore. I don't know where my mom is, or whether she's alive or dead— I'd like to at least find out someday, but I guess I never will.

Now Arba climbs up onto my lap. Poor Arba. Her mother came to America from Albania looking for a better life, but died of pneumonia. At least one day she will know where *her* mother is. When she's older, I'll make *sure* she knows.

"I know what Khalil's daddy looks like," Nestor says, hitting Khalil on the head.

"Yeah—how do you know?" Khalil riffs back.

"He's got a big coconut head—like you!"

"Yeah—well, we know your father probably has a big mouth, Nestlé's Quik," I tell Nestor.

Corky and Twinkie start giggling. Arba has fallen asleep on my lap, so I take her into her bedroom and put her in bed. I kiss her on the cheeks, and she whispers, "Good night, Do-reedy."

Chapter 2

As I lie on my pillow, I can't stop thinking about that runaway boy, Paulo Rivera. Why did he tell all those lies? I wonder if he was just trying to pull an okeydokey and get money out of people by making them feel sorry for him. Who wouldn't feel sorry for a kid hiking, biking, and sailing 2,000 miles just to find his father, right?

When they found him, the reporter said, he had $150 in his pockets. Tossing in my bed, I decide I would *never* go looking for my family, you know what I'm saying? I don't care where my mother and father are. They obviously don't love me, or I wouldn't be here.

I can feel myself starting to cry, but I get mad

instead. I'm tired of crying about stupid people who don't care about me. All of a sudden, I start crying anyway—but I think it's because I'm crying for Paulo. They shouldn't put him in a foster home—he must feel so scared right now. Why don't they just let him go back home to his aunt?

She doesn't want him anymore—that's probably why. That thought makes me angry, and I peek out from behind the pillow to see if Monie sees me crying.

She's just gotten home from her boyfriend Hector's house. Now she's sitting at the dresser, writing something—probably a stupid love letter to Hector, because I know she *never* does her homework. She's already been left back once, and she hates me because I got skipped twice. (I'm only twelve, but my crew doesn't know I'm so young—they think I'm fourteen like them, and I'm too afraid to tell them the truth. They'd probably never want to speak with me again, let alone chill with me!)

I cover my face with the pillow again, because the light from the lamp is bothering me. Then, all of a sudden, I find myself blurting out, "Do you ever think about your mother?"

The Cheetah Girls

Monie looks at me like I've lost my mind. "No," she says, getting an attitude, "and I don't know why you're lying there thinking about something so *stupid*."

Chantelle doesn't say anything; she just keeps popping her gum. What was I thinking about, talking to Monie? Her brain is on permanent vacation, you know? She doesn't understand anything. Neither does Chantelle. And my other foster sisters are too young. I wish I had a *real* sister like the twins. They have each other.

Well, actually, I do have a real sister. We were together in my first foster home. But she got to stay there, and I didn't, and that's the last I ever saw or heard from her.

Thank goodness for the Cheetah Girls. Having my crew—especially Chanel—is as close to having sisters as I'll ever get. Even so, it's not the same as having a real one. . . .

I'm in an apartment, and this pretty brown lady is showing me all her beautiful clothes. "You can come live with me and pick out all the clothes you want to wear," she says.

It's a really big apartment, and there are lots and lots of beautiful clothes everywhere. I start trying on some of the clothes, but they're all too big for me.

"Don't worry, when you grow up, you can wear these clothes, because I'll give them all to you," the pretty lady says. I ask her why. She tells me, "I'm your mother, that's why."

I start crying, and I hug her. She is so tall, and her skin is smooth chocolate. When she smiles, she looks like a movie star with really white teeth.

I don't even feel mad at her anymore. . . .

The noise from a car alarm wakes me up from my dream. I look at the clock and see that it's seven in the morning—time for me to get up and go to my Saturday morning vocal and dance lessons at Drinka Champagne Conservatory.

I walk to the bathroom, but somebody is in it. "Hurry up!" I yell, tapping my knuckles on the door.

I wonder who the lady in the dream was. She didn't look like anybody I know.

Maybe it *was* my mother. Maybe I'm psychic or something, like Chanel, and her father's girl-friend, Princess Pamela, who has a fortune-telling parlor.

The Cheetah Girls

Leaning against the bathroom door in a trance, I daydream about what my mother looks like. I guess I *would* like to know. She's probably pretty, and brown-skinned—and too busy to take care of me.

Suddenly I realize that I forgot to do my biology homework! I never space out like that. What was I supposed to be reading? That's right—the chapter on DNA—the stuff to do with genetics.

I'm in such a trance that when Twinkie opens up the bathroom door, I fall inside the doorway. She giggles and covers her head to keep me from falling on her. "Big cheetah bobo, you going to dance class now?" she asks, peering up at me.

"Yeah."

"I wish I could go. I wanna be a Cheetah Girl too," Twinkie says, pleadingly.

She always makes me feel so guilty about being in the Cheetah Girls. It's true I spend less time with her these days. And now she wants to be a part of what I'm doing.

"You know how you like to draw all those beautiful butterflies?" I say as I wash my face and hands.

"Yeah," Twinkie says.

"Well, dancing is what *I* like to do—and now, I'm singing too." I know she doesn't get it.

"Yeah, but I wanna dance and sing, too—if you'll let me!"

"You can dance and sing, Twinkie—if you want to do something badly enough, there's nobody in the world can stop you, least of all me. I'll tell you what—we're gonna find out if you can do something at school—"

"I wanna do it with *you!*" Twinkie insists, giggling and whining at the same time, like she always does.

"You can't."

"Okay, you big Cheetah bunny—I'm gonna flush you down the toilet!"

I tickle Twinkie, then run out of there and back into the bedroom to get dressed. I love going to Drinka Champagne Conservatory for vocal and dance classes—it's the bomb, and we always have a lotta fun, too. We are the Cheetah Girls, of course, and that means all five of us meet there—unlike during the week, when we go to separate schools. Aqua and Angie just got transferred to the Performing Arts League, which is an annex of LaGuardia

The Cheetah Girls

Performing Arts School—they're right next door to each other near Lincoln Center, and both of them are dope performing arts schools. As for me, Galleria, and Chanel, we all go to Fashion Industries East together.

As I'm running out the door, I feel around my neck, and realize I forgot to put on my Cheetah Girls choker, so I run back inside my room to get it. We made the Cheetah Girl chokers ourselves. We bought cheetah-printed strips of suede, then glued metal letters on them to spell the words GROWL POWER. The chokers are really dope looking, and they hold together fine—*now*.

At first, when we were trying to sell them, a lot of the lettering fell off. It was totally embarrassing, and I don't even want to talk about it. It's over, thank goodness. Now I actually *enjoy* wearing my choker. It tells the world who and what I am—"Do' Re Mi" Rogers, a Cheetah Girl with Ferocious Flava!

"Can we make a butterfly dress later?" Twinkie asks me, following me into the room.

"Yeah, later."

See, for Thanksgiving, the kids in Twinkie's school are making costumes, and Twinkie

24

wants to be a butterfly instead of a turkey—
even though her teacher says she has to stay
with the theme of Thanksgiving.

That's Twinkie for you. I told her to tell him
that she's one of the butterflies who came with
the first settlers to Plymouth Rock or something. She liked that idea.

"Twinkie, I need you to do something for
me."

"Okay."

"Mrs. Tattle, our caseworker, is coming over
at two o'clock—so I won't be back here in time
to get everybody ready. I want you to wear
your pink sweater with the pom-poms. Would
you do that for me?"

"Okay. Bye, pom-pom poot-butt!"

"I'm gonna get you later for that, Twinkie," I
chuckle as I put the Cheetah Girl choker
around my neck. Twinkie is still standing next
to me, staring.

"Twink—do you think these chokers are big
enough?"

"Yeah—you look like a big Cheetah Gorilla!"

"No, seriously—is the band wide enough?"

She shakes her head, then blurts out, "How
come I can't have one?"

That makes me feel really bad. How come I was only thinking about myself?

I touch the metal letters on the choker again. I can feel the letters spelling GROWL POWER. We must have it, all right, or Def Duck Records wouldn't be interested in putting us in the studio with big cheese producer Mouse Almighty to cut some tracks. I wonder when it's gonna happen. Every day we hope to hear something, but so far, *nada*.

I yell good-bye to Mrs. Bosco, who is sitting at the kitchen table with Corky, then give Arba a big hug. Twinkie is right at my heels.

"I'm counting on you, Cheetah Rita Butterfly," I whisper to her. Rita is Twinkie's real name, but I think it's her nickname—not Twinkie, but the one I gave her, Butterfly—that really makes her spread her wings.

Chapter 3

Miss Winnie, the receptionist at Drinka Champagne's Conservatory, gives me a big smile when she sees me. "Dorinda, how you doin'?" she asks, like she really wants to know.

I can't believe how nice everybody is to me here at the Conservatory—and I haven't even paid one ducket for anything! That's because Drinka (who founded this conservatory for divettes-in-training like the Cheetah Girls) gave me a full one-year scholarship. Miss Winnie even put me in Vocal 201, instead of 101, so I could be with my crew.

See, Galleria and Chanel have been coming to Drinka's for two years now, and Angie and

Aqua could sing like (almost) divas even before we met them. I'm a good dancer, but I'm still learning to sing. More important, next to the rest of the Cheetah Girls, I still feel like a wanna-be star in the jiggy jungle, just like the words in the song Bubbles wrote.

"I'm just fine, Miss Winnie. Are the rest of the Cheetah Girls here yet?"

"Yes. And you girls better take a look at the bulletin board, too. There's something you may be interested in," Miss Winnie adds, winking at me.

That must mean there's something dope, like an audition or something. See, sometimes casting directors who are looking for young talent contact Drinka's Conservatory, so the school puts up notices on the bulletin board. Drinka was the queen of disco back in the day, and she still has mad "connects" all over the place.

I wonder what's jumping down. But I don't get a chance to check it out right away, because it's time for class to begin!

"Dorinda—*qué linda!*" exclaims Chanel when I walk into the studio. The Cheetah Girls are all so hyped these days, ever since we had our big meeting with Def Duck Records. Like I said, they're gonna put us in a studio with big cheese producer, Mouse Almighty, to cut a few songs for a possible demo. We don't know *when* it's going to go down, but we are definitely "in the house with Mouse," as Bubbles puts it.

I hug Chanel first. Even though I'm down with all the Cheetah Girls, I definitely feel the closest with Chanel. We have a lot in common. I mean, her pops is gone, and she and her mom don't exactly seem to be watching the same *Telemundo* television show, if you know what I'm saying. Her mom doesn't want Chanel to just be herself. I mean, Chanel may not be good at math or spelling, but she is really sweet. She knows how to make people feel like she cares about them, and how to make you laugh—and that counts for a lot —especially in our crew.

"Guess who's here? It's Do' Re Mi—so now we can flip it like posse!" Bubbles chants, giving me a Cheetah Girls handshake. She has on a hot-pink sweater and pink lipstick, which makes her look kinda like her nickname—a juicy piece of bubble gum!

"Galleria, you heard anything else from the Def Duck peeps?" I ask. All this waiting just to hear when we can kick it in the studio makes me so anxious. I just want us to move and groove already, ayiight?

"*Nada*," Galleria says, shaking her head. I can tell she's on the anxious tip, too. "I can't wait till we can get into a studio. I mean *enuf* with the powder puff!"

"I heard that," I groan.

"Daddy doesn't understand why they just don't give us a record deal," Aquanette says, her eyes popping wide. "I told him the music business is not like the pest control business—you can't just expect a roach to crawl up into a roach motel and be done with it!"

I chuckle at Aqua's joke. The twins have definitely gotten more live, if you know what I'm saying.

After our class, Drinka pulls all five of us aside. "Now listen, Cheetah Girls, there's a notice upstairs I want you to look at—the 'Battle of the Divettes' competition."

Chanel jumps up and down like a Mexican jumping bean.

"Now, a lot of the students are gonna try out for it, but I think this one has your name written all over it—'divettes.' Drinka's red lip gloss is shining like a neon sign as she breaks into a big smile, showing off the biggest, whitest teeth I've ever seen. "Send in your tape and see if you get an audition for it."

"What kind of tape?" Bubbles asks, looking at us.

"Don't tell me you haven't made a videotape of yourselves performing yet?" Drinka asks, like she can't believe it. Suddenly, I feel like a wanna-be all over again.

"Dag on, I guess we haven't," Aqua pipes up, looking sullen.

"Well, run out and make one," Drinka commands us. "*Au revoir, mes chéries.*" Drinka lays on the thick French accent, the way Chanel's mom, Juanita, does.

"*Au revoir,*" Chanel coos.

"*Croissant,*" giggles Bubbles, and kisses Drinka on the cheek.

Drinka was right. The "Battle of the Divettes" competition does seem like it has our names written on it. The headline on the posting reads: *If you think you're fierce, call and submit your tape. (Photo and bio optional).*

"Oh, lawdy, lawd," Angie says, grabbing her sister Aqua's hand and continuing to read the listing. "Unsigned talent who make 'The Grade' will compete on air. MTV will finance and air a professionally produced video of the grand prize winner!"

"Remember those girls—'In the Dark?'" Aqua asks. "You know—the leader of the group wears a fake eye patch, and the other girls have got those monkey-head canes?"

"Yeah," Angie says, scrunching up her nose. "I told you I don't like them. She's trying to look like Zorro, with that black eye patch covered with rhinestones." I think they're too flashy for the twins, if you know what I'm saying.

"Yes, we know what you think, Miz Anginette, but you know how she got to floss that eye patch in the first place? By winning the grand prize on *The Grade*," Bubbles says exasperated. "Now those girls have it made in the shade."

"Is that right?" Angie responds sheepishly.

"If *they* can get a deal by thumping around with those wack-a-doodle-do monkey canes and that fake eye patch action, then imagine what a bunch of cheetah-fied divettes could get?" Galleria continues. "We should pounce right to first place just by licking our paws on the air, you know what I'm saying?"

"Okay, Miss Galleria, we know what you're saying," Aqua says, cracking a smile now that she gets Galleria's point.

"I'd enter the 'Battle of the Divettes' contest even if they were just giving away Goofy Grape sodas for first prize!" I say, chuckling. The whole idea sounds good to me—as long as we're not actually signed by Def Duck, we're still eligible.

"I know that's right," Aqua pipes up, confirming what I was thinking without blinking.

We continue reading the listing, and find out that the Battle of the Divettes competition is being held at the Apollo Theatre uptown. We look at each other, and I know we're all thinking the same thing. *Oh, no, say it ain't so. Not another Nightmare on 125th Street!*

See, the Cheetah Girls performed in the Apollo Amateur Hour contest and we *lost*, to a pair of wanna-be rappers called Stak Chedda— and believe me, they weren't "betta." I think we're still hurting from that disaster.

As usual, though, Galleria is hyping us up. "You know what they say—lightning never strikes twice in the same place."

"Yeah, that's true—but it don't say nothing about *losing*!" Aqua blurts out.

"Don't be radikkio. It's a new day and a new situation, so let's just go with the flow and act like we know," Galleria says, whipping out her Kitty Kat notebook and scribbling down all the information.

"But, *mamacita*, the contest is next Saturday!" Chanel says. "How are we gonna get a video-tape made in time to send it in and meet the deadline—by calling 1-800-ALADDIN?" She twirls her hair anxiously. Chanel always twirls her hair when she gets nervous.

"No, Chuchie, we're gonna ask Mom to help us," Galleria says, whipping out her Miss Wiggy StarWac cell phone. I wish I had a cell phone—it's so cool to be able to flex and floss on the move, you know what I'm saying?

"I'm hungry—what time is it?" Aqua asks, licking her juicy lips.

Looking at my watch, I almost shriek—"It's one-thirty!"

"Do' Re Mi, *qué pasa, mamacita*?" Chanel asks, concerned.

"I've gotta be home," I say, getting

embarrassed. Why should I tell them I have to go home because a stupid caseworker is coming over to my house? *I hate that.* All of a sudden, I feel like Cinderella or something.

Chanel gives me a look with her big, goo-goo brown eyes, like, "why won't you tell me?"

"Um, my caseworker, Mrs. Tattle, is coming over today," I say, feeling my face get warm. I keep on talking, because I'm getting more and more embarrassed. "I don't know why she's coming over on a Saturday, but I've got to be there."

Chanel puts her arm around me. "I hope Mrs. Tattle's got a *boca grande*. With that name, she'd better be talking and sticking up for you, *está bien?*"

"I guess so," I say, looking over at Galleria; but I'm relieved when I see that she isn't really listening to us, because she's on the phone, sorta fighting with her mom, Ms. Dorothea. At least I feel off the hook. . . .

"I hope Mrs. Tattle doesn't stay long, you know what I'm saying?" I confide to my crew.

"I know that's right," Aqua says, looking at me with real concern. The twins come from a close family—and I understand that they watch each other's back. They probably think my situation is so strange.

Little do they know about the ways of the Big Apple. There are a *lot* of foster kids here—something like forty thousand—so I'm not alone, you know what I'm saying? Sometimes they have articles in the newspaper about foster kids like me.

"Can't the caseworkers leave you alone, now that Mrs. Bosco adopted you?" Aqua asks, hesitating. Suddenly, I realize that I haven't told my crew about the adoption mix-up yet. Omigod, what should I do? Now I feel like Chanel—always opening my *boca grande* for *nada*—for nothing!

I take a deep breath, and fiddle with the straps on my cheetah backpack. Even though it's emptier than usual, all of a sudden my backpack feels like a "magilla gorilla" on my back.

I'm so tired of all the fib-eronis I've been telling my crew. I know it's gonna catch up to me one day—and I guess today is the day, okay?

"Mrs. Bosco thought the adoption went

through, but it didn't," I say, hemming and hawing. I'm *not* going to tell them that she can't read or write. No way, José.

"Really?" Chanel asks me, like I'm joking, her big brown eyes opening wide like she doesn't believe me.

"Really, Chanel. I wouldn't joke about something like that," I say, trying to figure out how I can explain Mrs. Bosco's mistake to them. It wasn't *all* her fault. "They couldn't find my mother to get her to sign over her parental rights, or something like that. I don't know!"

Now Aqua hugs me. Galleria is off the phone, and she catches a whiff of my so-called adoption drama. "So you're *not* legally adopted?" she asks, surprised.

"No, I'm not adopted, okay?" I huff, but Galleria is like a dog with a bone—she just won't leave it alone.

"But Mrs. Bosco is not gonna give you up or anything, is she?"

I don't even want to *think* about that. She said she wouldn't, but what do I know? "I don't know, Galleria."

They get really quiet, which makes me mad

uncomfortable, so I change the subject. "So what did your mom say?"

"Um, she wanted to know why we were just finding out about the contest," Galleria says slowly. "I told her that's how this whole show-biz thing flows, you know? It moves on a dime and our time."

"It does say a 'home-made video,' though," Angie says, trying to be helpful.

"Yeah, that's what I told her—so we've just gotta hook up the lights-camera-action situation on the Q.T.," Galleria says, like she's not stressing it. "Mom thinks my dad may have a video camera. He's over at one of the contractors' right now." Galleria's parents own a clothing factory and boutique called Toto in New York . . . Fun in Diva Sizes. I guess the contractors are their suppliers or something.

"See, I know Granddaddy Walker has a video camera," Aqua says, thinking out loud. Granddaddy Walker owns a funeral parlor in Houston.

"He's not videotaping those dead people in the coffins, is he, *mamacita*?" Chanel asks, getting the spookies.

"Yes, Chanel—he especially *loves* the part

after he puts the embalming fluid in the body, and the dead corpse jumps up on the table when the rigor mortis sets in!"

I start chuckling, because I feel so much better that we aren't talking about my home situation.

"That's what really happens!" Aqua claims, bugging her eyes.

"It's true—we saw it one time when we were little," Angie adds, giggling. No wonder the twins love horror movies so much!

We all are in a good mood now. "Well, let's get rolling on 'Operation Videotape!'" Bubbles commands. "We're on a roll now, *girlitas*!"

Chapter 4

Mrs. Tattle is waiting in my living room when I get home. She looks kinda tired, and her clothes are all wrinkled. She even has a run in her stocking, and a spot on her pink blouse (it looks like tomato sauce), but I guess I'd better not say anything. She is pretty nice as caseworkers go, and I don't want to embarrass her. Besides, caseworkers write up recommendations about whether you get to stay in your foster home or not—so they have a lot of power over kids like me, and the last thing you want to do is make a bad impression.

"Sit down, Dorinda—take a load off," Mrs. Bosco says, stroking the hair on her wig in the front. I'm so glad she is wearing her special wig. See, Princess Pamela (the girlfriend of Chanel's dad) styled Mrs. Bosco's wig for my so-called adoption party. Princess Pamela is a dope hairdresser, and a psychic, too! Now, Mrs. Bosco keeps the wig in a net in her wig drawer, and only takes it out for special occasions. I wish she would wear it all the time, because the other ones look, well, kinda fake, if you know what I'm saying.

"Can I get you something to drink?" Mrs. Bosco asks Mrs. Tattle, but I know she will probably say, "No, thank you." She always does. Mrs. Tattle is usually in a hurry. Mrs. Bosco says the caseworkers who work for the city—as opposed to private foster care agencies—always have too big a caseload, and they don't get paid enough to deal with all the headaches that come with the territory. Mrs. Bosco must be right, 'cuz Mrs. Tattle has bags under her eyes that look more like suitcases!

"How are you today, Dorinda?" Mrs. Tattle asks me, reaching over to open her briefcase, which is right next to her on the floor.

I'm trying not to stare at the railroad run in her panty hose. I wonder how high up her leg it goes? When I'm older, I'm going to carry a briefcase like Mrs. Tattle, so I can look important, too.

Mrs. Tattle seems kinda uptight. The way she is sitting so straight on the couch, you'd think she was in the Oval Office in the White House or something. The couch in our living room is covered with faded yellow-flowered tapestry, and the seat cushions are well worn. I think more people have sat on our couch than in the Oval Office, if you know what I'm saying.

"I'm fine," I say, smiling and showing off my dimples, so Mrs. Tattle will feel more comfortable. I want her to think everything is "hunky chunky." I'm also anxious to find out why she's visiting us on a Saturday.

"Mrs. Bosco told me the good news about your record deal," Mrs. Tattle says, trying to sound cheerful.

"Well, it's not exactly a record deal, but we're going to get to cut a few songs for a demo tape for the record company," I explain carefully. I'm always trying to be honest about the Cheetah Girls situation—like I said earlier, we may have "growl power," but so far, we are still a bunch of wanna-be stars in the jiggy jungle.

"Well, it must have been exciting for you to

go to Los Angeles," Mrs. Tattle says, trying to make everything seem really hunky chunky, too.

"It was the dopest dope experience I ever had in my life!" I say, because I don't want to let Mrs. Tattle down. It *was* pretty dope—but there were ups and downs, if you want to know the honest truth.

"Well, now that's more like the Dorinda I know!" she says, her voice screeching because she is talking too high. (Now that I'm taking vocal lessons, I notice *everything* about people's voices. It's really kinda strange.)

Mrs. Tattle keeps smiling at me and Mrs. Bosco. Twinkie is smiling at Mrs. Tattle, and sitting in the armchair with her hand under her chin. "And how are you, Rita?" Mrs. Tattle asks, her face brightening up. Twinkie makes everybody smile.

"I'm okay," Twinkie responds, without moving her hand from her chin. Kenya just sits on the couch looking down at her shoes. I'm proud of Twinkie, because at least she got Kenya to wear matching socks. Topwe, Chantelle, Khalil, and Nestor look nice, too.

"Dorinda, can you sing something for me?"

Mrs. Tattle asks, catching me off guard.

"Not right now," I say, getting embarrassed. None of the other caseworkers have ever asked me to sing for them before.

Kenya throws me a look, like, "Why don't you just do what Mrs. Tattle wants?" For someone who whines so much, Kenya gets awfully quiet when the caseworker visits.

I guess it wouldn't hurt me to sing for Mrs. Tattle. Maybe she thinks I'm just making the whole thing up about being in a singing group called the Cheetah Girls. I'm sure she must have put that in her reports. She's always writing things down when she visits.

"Um, okay, lemme see," I say, trying to be nice to Mrs. Tattle. "I'll sing you the song that Bubbles wrote."

"Bubbles?" Mrs. Tattle asks, like she's kinda curious.

"Oh, she's the leader of our group—that's her nickname. Her real name is Galleria Garibaldi."

"Oh," Mrs. Tattle says, nodding her head. "That's an interesting name."

"Um, yeah, her mother is a fashion designer, and she named Bubbles, um, Galleria, after the

44

mall in Houston," I say. I start giggling, warming up to Mrs. Tattle because I see her eyes sparkling a little. "Her father is Italian—from Italy—so that's where she got her last name."

"Yes—Garibaldi was a popular hero in Italy," Mrs. Tattle says.

I just keep smiling, because I'm not sure about Italian history. I'd better ask Bubbles before I go blabbing my mouth, so I decide I'd better sing and get it over with. "Um, okay, here's the song that Bubbles wrote. It's called, 'Wanna-be Stars in the Jiggy Jungle.'"

"Oh, that's cute!" Mrs. Tattle says, scribing stuff down in a folder—which I know is my case file.

I smile at Twinkie. She loves to join in on the chorus of this song. I clear my throat and start singing the first verse:

"*Some people walk with a panther*
or strike a buffalo stance
that makes you wanna dance.

Other people flip the script
on the day of the jackal
that'll make you cackle.

But peeps like me
got the Cheetah Girl groove
that makes your body move
like wanna-be stars in the jiggy jungle.

The jiggy jiggy jungle!
The jiggy jiggy jungle!"

Sure enough, Twinkie and Topwe join in for the chorus and the B verse, making a whole lot of noise—but at least it's fun:

"So don't make me bungle
my chance to rise for the prize
and show you who we are
in the jiggy jiggy jungle!
The jiggy jiggy jungle!"

Mrs. Tattle starts clapping enthusiastically. I'm so glad that I made her feel better. That's what I love most about singing—seeing how happy it makes people.

"Where *is* the jiggy jungle?" Mrs. Tattle asks me. I can tell she really is interested now.

"Bubbles says it's this magical, cheetah-licious place inside of every dangerous, scary, crowded city, where dreams come true—oh, and where every cheetah has its day." I get embarrassed, because I suddenly realize maybe Mrs. Tattle thinks the whole thing is kinda cuckoo.

But instead, she looks at me with tiny tears forming in her eyes. "I'm so glad you found a friend like Bubbles," Mrs. Tattle says softly. Then she adds hesitantly, "I remember reading in the reports that you had trouble connecting with other kids."

That makes me embarrassed. I didn't know one of the caseworkers put that in their report! They are so *nosy*!

Out of the corner of my eye, I see Mrs. Bosco nodding her head. "Yes, that's right. Dorinda has really changed a lot, now that she is in this group with the Cheetah Girls."

"This is really great, Dorinda," Mrs. Tattle exclaims.

I guess it's true. I never did have a lot of friends before, except when I was younger and I used to skateboard with Sugar Bear. Otherwise I kept to myself, hiding in my books or helping with the other kids at home.

Mrs. Tattle shifts her body on the couch. "Um, Dorinda, I came here today especially to see you. I wanted to talk to you about something before I go on vacation."

I notice Mrs. Tattle looking over at Mrs. Bosco like they've already talked about something.

"Um, Mrs. Bosco—would it be okay if you and I and Dorinda talked in private?"

"Of course," Mrs. Bosco says, smiling. "Y'all can go to your rooms," she tells the other kids. "Rita, baby, can you take Arba into the bedroom and show her how to draw those butterflies?"

"Did you draw some new ones, Rita?" Mrs. Tattle asks Twinkie.

"Yup—big, fat butterflies with purple eyes!" Twinkie says proudly.

"Would you show them to me later?" Mrs. Tattle asks Twinkie.

"Uh-huh."

Now I feel nervous again. Singing made me forget about everything for a while. Mrs. Tattle shuffles some papers, then looks at me.

"Um, Dorinda, did you know that you have a sister?" Mrs. Tattle asks me hesitantly.

"Um, yeah—Jazmine. She lives with my first foster mother, Mrs. Parkay," I respond.

I wonder why Mrs. Tattle looks so puzzled. She rifles through some of her papers again. Mrs. Bosco and I just sit quietly, waiting for her to finish.

"Oh, I see. Yes. Jazmine Jones. She was a foster child in the first home you were in," Mrs. Tattle says, reading from a paper. Then, she looks up at me, and her voice gets very quiet. "But actually . . . she wasn't, um, your biological sister," she says.

"I didn't know that!" I gasp. What a stupid thing to say, but it's all I can think of. I mean, all this time, I thought Jazmine was my *real* sister—and that mean Mrs. Parkay gave me away and kept Jazmine, separating us forever.

Obviously, I know more about the other kids' records than my own. I wonder what else is in that file Mrs. Tattle is holding. . . .

"How come she, um, Jazmine, got to stay with Mrs. Parkay?" I ask, my cheeks burning.

"Um, I don't know, Dorinda," Mrs. Tattle says. Embarrassed, she starts shuffling her papers some more. "Perhaps because Jazmine was younger than you . . . or maybe Mrs.

Parkay only wanted one child. I'll have to look it up in the files and get back to you on that. But at any rate, you and Jazmine are not biological sisters."

I can tell Mrs. Tattle is trying not to hurt my feelings. She probably knows why Mrs. Parkay gave me away, but she isn't saying anything. "Oh, that's okay. I was just asking," I say, getting defensive. "It's not important or anything."

I guess Mrs. Parkay just didn't love me enough—same as with my birth mother. Mr. and Mrs. Bosco are the only ones who *really* love me. That's why, in my heart, they're my *real* parents—whether I ever get adopted by them or not.

But now I'm really curious as to why Mrs. Tattle's here.

"Dorinda," she says, clearing her throat. "Um, Dorinda, what I started to say before was, you *do* have a biological sister. Well—*half* sister, actually. According to the records, you and Tiffany were born to the same mother, but you have different fathers."

Tiffany. I sit there, hearing the sound of it repeat and repeat inside my head. I have a half sister—a real one—and her name is Tiffany.

I look at Mrs. Bosco. I wonder if she knew about this before now—but I can't tell by the look on her face if she did or not.

"Her name's Tiffany?"

"Yes, Tiffany Twitty. She was adopted by the Twittys when she was a baby, and they changed her name."

"What was her name before that?" I ask curiously, and I'm thinking any name's gotta be better than one that sounds like a cuckoo bird.

"Oh, I'll have to look that up," Mrs. Tattle says, and now she sounds like a caseworker, instead of nice like before.

"How old is she?" I ask.

"Eleven. One year younger than you," Mrs. Tattle says with a blank face. "Well, Dorinda . . ." She clears her throat again, and I know there's more to come. "The reason why I'm telling you all this is—because Tiffany wants to meet you."

I feel a cold chill ripple down my body. All of a sudden, I feel sad and scared. Just a few weeks ago, I thought I was getting adopted— that I'd finally have a real family for the first time in my life. Now I find out Jazmine wasn't my real sister—and that I have a half sister named Tiffany Twitty, who's already been adopted!

It's all too much information trying to squeeze into my head at the same time. Suddenly I'm not sure I want to know any more about Tiffany—not yet, anyway.

And then, a familiar daydream comes to me—my mother is smiling at me in the clouds, while I'm dancing for her. I know it sounds stupid, but for some reason, the image keeps coming to me.

"Dorinda?" Mrs. Tattle says, trying to get my attention. "If you need to think about this—"

"I'm sorry—I was just thinking about things," I tell her. "I don't know what to do. . . ."

"Dorinda, you don't have to decide now," Mrs. Tattle says, being nice again.

I look up at Mrs. Bosco. She is nodding her head and smiling at me, like "Go ahead, don't be scared. I'm here for you."

"No, I *want* to meet her," I tell Mrs. Tattle.

She seems relieved. "Well, it would be better if I introduce the two of you—just to make sure everything, um, goes okay," she says very officiously, like a caseworker again. "Let's see," she says, looking in the files again. "You both seem to like skating. . . ."

"Skate*boarding*?" I say, correcting Mrs. Tattle.

"Well, I mean, you like skateboarding, and Tiffany likes Rollerblading. We could go to Central Park, perhaps—"

"Okay," I say with a shrug. "Whatever." Like I don't care how we meet, or how it goes.

But I do care. What if we don't like each other? What if she's mean, or something? What if she hates me? It's a good thing Mrs. Bosco puts her hand on my shoulder at that moment. She must sense that I'm about to back right out of this whole thing.

This is all such a trip—the sister I thought was my sister is not—but now I find out someone else is my *real* sister. . . .

Chapter 5

I can't believe all the stuff that is going down today! Before I go meet Tiffany and Mrs. Tattle at noon, right by the fountain in Central Park, I have to go meet the Cheetah Girls at Ms. Dorothea's store, Toto in New York . . . Fun in Diva Sizes.

Today's the day we're going to make the videotape to send in to the "Battle of the Divettes" competition. It turns out Bubbles's dad, Mr. Garibaldi, has a professional-quality video camera he keeps in storage!

"He wanted to be a filmmaker when he was younger," Bubbles tells me proudly. We're in the back of the boutique, changing into our Cheetah Girls costumes.

Ms. Dorothea plops down a platter of sandwiches on the shelves where hats are displayed. The sandwiches look really fancy, and I'm afraid to touch them.

"Darling, go on—take one. It's Black Forest ham and brie, laced with honey mustard."

I don't know what Black Forest ham is, but it sounds exotic, so I dig in—and it is *mm-mm* good! I'm munching away, and I look at Ms. Dorothea with a nervous smile.

Why am I nervous? Well, partly, it's the videotaping. But mostly, it's because I'm meeting Tiffany right afterward—and I haven't said a word to anybody! Not even Chanel—and I tell Chanel *everything*.

I'm wondering if I should tell Ms. Dorothea about Tiffany. I *know* Ms. Dorothea would understand how confused I feel about everything. At my "adoption" party, she was crying, and she told me everything about her missing mother.

No . . . I think it's better if I don't say anything—not yet, anyway. Not till I know what's the deal-io.

Bubbles's dog Toto (they named the store for him) is lying with his nose pressed to the floor.

Toto is the dopest dog in the jiggy jungle. Right now, he looks like a fluffy pancake.

"Hi, Toto," I coo, and he immediately cocks his head and patters over, rubbing his body against my knees. He is wearing the cutest outfit. He's gonna be featured in our video, but that's not why he's all dressed up. See, Galleria and her mom love to make outfits for him anytime there's leftover fabric. That dog has more costumes than *we* do—well, so far, anyway. This one's a yellow-net tutu, with cheetah ribbons streaming all over the place.

"Ooh, I've got a dope idea," Chanel says, fondling the cheetah ribbons on Toto's tutu. "I could put these on one of *my* tutus." Chanel used to take ballet lessons. She stopped her ballet training because Galleria didn't want to do it anymore—and those two are the dynamic duo: whatever one does, the other has to do. They're "thicker than forty thieves," as the rap song "Don't Bite the Flavor that You Savor," says. Anyway, I can tell Chanel still loves ballet, even though she pretends she doesn't.

Toto rolls over on his back and puts his front paws in the air. "He really likes getting his stomach rubbed," I chuckle.

"Yeah, and he'd be happy if you alternated it with fanning his fur and feeding him some grapes!" Ms. Dorothea humphs. "All Toto needs now is a harem." She leads us to the front of the store, where she poses us against the cheetah-wallpapered wall.

"What's a harem?" Angie asks.

"It's lots of pretty girls who run around with veils, and with their belly buttons sticking out, pampering the whims of horribly rich princes," Ms. Dorothea explains.

Chanel lets out a giggle, then starts wiggling her middle and pretending to fan Toto with her scarf. See, Chanel's mom, Juanita, takes belly-dancing lessons all the time now. Her boyfriend is this rich businessman who lives in Paris, France. Chanel calls him Mr. Tycoon. I think Chanel's mom is trying to be his one-woman harem, 'cuz she sure is working hard at those belly-dancing lessons.

"Chanel, you'd better feed him something, or he's gonna bite you," Ms. Dorothea chuckles.

"*Madrina*, I'm not giving him my sandwich, *está bien?*" Chanel says, picking up her sandwich and gobbling it down.

Mr. Garibaldi is videotaping everything we

do. He seems excited—kind of like a kid with a new toy.

"I always wanted to be like Fellini," Mr. Garibaldi tells us.

"Who is Fellini?" I ask curiously.

"Ah, Dor-i-n-d-a, *bella*, Federico Fellini was the greatest Italian movie director that *ever* lived. *È vero, cara.* It's true."

"Darling, he made a fabulous movie called *La Dolce Vita*," Ms. Dorothea pipes in, looking over at Mr. Garibaldi with stars in her eyes. "The first time I saw it was with my Franco, and I've been living it ever since."

Franco is part of Mr. Garibaldi's first name—Francobollo, which means "stamp" in Italian. I'm not sure what *la dolce vita* means. As if reading my mind, Galleria looks at me and says, amused, "It means, 'the sweet life.'"

"Word," I say chuckling. Mr. and Mrs. Garibaldi sure look like they have *la dolce vita*! They are so cute together—even if she is a head taller than he is.

"Okay, Cheetah Girls, stop eating, and let's get to work," Mr. Garibaldi commands us.

The five of us are wearing the cheetah jumpsuits Ms. Dorothea made for us when we gave our very first performance—last Halloween night at the Cheetah-Rama Club.

Ms. Dorothea seems to be having fun playing makeup artist and hairdresser. She keeps *poufing* us with powder, and fussing with our hair.

"Everything okay?" Ms. Dorothea asks, looking at me amused.

"Tutti frutti!" I heckle back. Galleria is so lucky to have Ms. Dorothea for a mother—but then, I guess I'm lucky too, having her as a manager.

"Then let's do it!" Chanel says.

The five of us strike a pose that satisfies both Mr. and Mrs. Garibaldi, and we begin singing "Wanna-be Stars in the Jiggy Jungle."

After we finish, Mr. Garibaldi yells, "Cut," just like a real movie director.

Galleria goes over and hugs him. "Thank you, Daddy. You're even better than Fellini. Now where's the linguini?"

Ms. Dorothea runs to the back to bring out the food. We dig into the linguini with clam sauce while Mr. Garibaldi puts his coat on. He's rushing over to the processing lab, then mailing off our videotape to Looking Good

Productions, so we don't miss the deadline for the "Battle of the Divettes" competition.

"Let's go to Manhattan Mall!" Chuchie says excitedly.

Suddenly, I get nervous. I didn't count on going anywhere with my crew after we made a tape. I haven't even told them about Tiffany— let alone that I'm going to meet her this afternoon.

"I have to go meet my, um, caseworker, at twelve o'clock," I say, embarrassed.

"I thought you met her yesterday," Galleria says, puzzled.

"Yeah, well, she's, um, going on vacation for a long time, so I have to see her again," I say, stammering.

Galleria puts her arm around me. I guess she feels sorry for me or something. I feel so stupid, but I'm just not ready to tell them about the sister situation. Maybe after I meet Tiffany—if everything goes well, that is.

I kiss everybody good-bye and anchor my skateboard under my arm.

"How come you have your skateboard with you?" Chanel asks, curious.

"I'm meeting Mrs. Tattle in Central Park

with, um, some other kids," I explain, feeling my face getting flushed.

"Maybe I could come with you and just hang out," Chanel says, her eyes looking hopeful. Now I really feel bad. Chanel has been wanting me to teach her skateboarding ever since we met. Luckily, Galleria and the twins aren't having it.

"Chuchie, that's all you need is to go kadoodling around on a skateboard, and you won't be a wanna-be star anymore—you'll just be seeing stars, 'cuz you'll hurt yourself!"

"*I* sure wouldn't want to try it," Aqua pipes up. "It looks *real* dangerous."

"Well, I guess I shouldn't come today, anyway, since you're meeting with your caseworker and all," Chanel says. "We'll go skateboarding soon, though, right? When it's just us two, and you can give me a lesson, *está bien?*"

"Word, *mamacita*," I say, chuckling.

Chanel's not quite over the disappointment yet, though. She touches the grip tape on my skateboard and follows the deck with her fingers. I can see Chanel is fascinated. That's one of the many things we have in common—she likes to move and groove with the wind as much as I do. She's athletic like me, too—I mean, she did all those years of ballet—and she could probably learn to skateboard pretty fast if I found the time to teach her.

"The kicktail on mine only has a slight angle," I explain. "It's the same in the front and back. This is the kind you get when you're into freestyle."

"Do you have to wear high-top sneakers?" Chanel asks, looking down at my sneaks.

"Yeah—with reinforcement on the side. You can really mess up regular sneakers when you do ollies or fakies—this way, you can keep your ankles tweaked." I know Chanel understands how important it is to protect your ankles because of her ballet training.

"Good, golly, what's an ollie?" Aqua asks, still munching on the linguini. When there's good food around, you practically have to pry the twins away from it with a crowbar, you know what I'm saying?

Chuckling, I put the skateboard down for a second to show them an ollie. "You hit the kicktail with your back foot, then you kinda jump."

"Whoa, Miss Dorinda, I don't want you to

take the mannequins in the window with you," Ms. Dorothea warns me. "Shouldn't you be wearing knee pads or something?"

"I usually do—but I lent my brother Khalil my board, and he lost all my safety equipment. So till I can afford some more . . . Anyway, it's only street boarding. I don't go very fast, or try to do any really fancy tricks."

"Okay, well just be careful. Those 'In the Dark' girls may be hobbling on canes for fun— but I don't want you needing one for real."

"I'll be careful," I reassure everyone. "Bye, y'all."

I leave the store, and set off for the subway station, on my way to meet the half sister I never knew I had.

Something tells me this is going to be the ride of a lifetime.

Chapter 6

When I get off the subway at Sixty-sixth Street and Broadway, I put my skateboard down on the sidewalk and skate into Central Park. I can't believe I'm going to meet my sister—my *real* sister, you know what I'm saying? I don't know whether I'm more thrilled or more scared!

"Coming through!" I yell politely, so this guy coming at me on a ten-speeder can leave me some room on the sidewalk. He's zooming past me, like he's a werewolf and his paws are on fire or something. Bicycle peeps are outta control in the Big Apple.

Once he passes, I jumpstart my stride with a few back kicks, and start cruising along the path that leads into the park.

A ferocious breeze blows my way, so I zip up my jacket, pick up my skateboard, and walk down the steep steps toward the famous fountain in Central Park. I wonder if Tiffany is tiny like me? That's how I'll know if she is *really* my sister, I think to myself, chuckling inside.

But I can't shake how badly I feel for not telling my crew about this whole drama. Now I'm quaking for faking, and I wish I could just turn back and hang with them at the Manhattan Mall, just like any other Sunday. But it's too late for that.

I see Mrs. Tattle standing by herself over by the pond area. I wave hello, then glance away, pretending that I'm looking at the ducks floating by on the dirty pond water.

I always feel self-conscious when I'm walking toward someone who's standing still. I feel like I'm gonna trip, or do something stupid, and then they won't like me anymore. Now I glance over at the people sitting in rowboats—aren't they cold? I wonder.

"Hi, Dorinda," Mrs. Tattle beams at me. "I see you brought your skateboard."

"Yeah, I boarded over from the subway

station," I say nervously, looking around. Next to me, a barefoot boy is sticking his toe in the brook. His mother glances at me, then turns back to her son and smiles. I can tell she is kinda poor, because her clothes look dirty. But at least *she* didn't give her son away. Suddenly, I feel sad about my situation. Why couldn't I have stayed with my mother from the beginning?

And where is Tiffany? I wonder. Maybe she didn't show up, after all.

As if reading my mind, Mrs. Tattle points to the hot dog vendor on the other side of the fountain, and says, "Tiffany is right over there, buying a hot dog. Would you like one?"

"No, thank you," I tell her. "Ms. Dorothea— Galleria's mom—made lunch for us," I respond. But the main reason is, I want to get a look at Tiffany before she sees me. That will give me a minute to check her out. Then, when she sees me, I can watch how she reacts to seeing me for the first time. I wonder if we look alike. . . .

In biology class in school, we're studying genetics—DNA and genes, and stuff like that. According to what our teacher says, you get half your genes from each parent. Half of who you are. So Tiffany and I will be half alike!

This is kinda exciting, after all. Scared as I am, I'm busy looking at the hot dog stand to see if I can pick out Tiffany. But I don't see anybody that looks remotely like she could be my sister.

What is Mrs. Tattle talking about? I look at her, just to make sure she hasn't gone cuckoo. I know she's supa busy with her caseload. Maybe she just goofed up; you know what I'm saying? Or maybe Tiffany went somewhere else in the park besides the hot dog stand.

Mrs. Tattle smiles at me nervously, then puts down her briefcase on the ground and folds her arms across her chest. I guess it must be kinda tiring, to carry a heavy briefcase around town all the time.

I wonder if Mrs. Tattle ever gets to have any fun, or what her husband is like. But I never ask caseworkers questions about their lives, because Mrs. Bosco says it's rude. She says, "They're just here to do their job, not to have us all up in their business."

"Here comes Tiffany," Mrs. Tattle says enthusiastically, as if she's announcing the arrival of a beauty contestant or something.

The Cheetah Girls

I look at the hot dog stand, to see who is walking in our direction. There's an older man with an overcoat full of holes and a feather in his hat, shuffling along like he's in a hurry. There is a group of little kids, running around in circles. And there's an old homeless lady, who is mumbling loudly to a group of pigeons while she scatters breadcrumbs. Mrs. Tattle might really be cuckoo like that lady, I think, and start panicking.

Then I see a cute, chubby girl with long, blond hair. She is wearing white shorts, kneepads, and Rollerblades. This girl is chomping down on a hot dog, and skating at the same time. *She must be freezing*, I say to myself. I mean, I'm shivering myself!

Now the blond girl is zooming closer to us, and smiling at Mrs. Tattle. Maybe she was talking to Mrs. Tattle before or something.

"Hi," the girl says to me, smiling. She wipes the onions from the corner of her mouth with a napkin. "It's great to meet you." She sticks out her hand to shake—and drops her hot dog with everything on it, right on my skateboard!

"Oh, no!" the girl gasps.

"Don't worry, Tiffany, I'll get it," Mrs. Tattle

says, bending down and trying to clean up the mess.

Hold up, I think, suddenly stiffening. I just thought I heard Mrs. Tattle call this girl Tiffany. That's my *sister's* name. But this girl is *white*!

Maybe Mrs. Tattle meant Tiffany is *going* to be my sister or something. No, that can't be. Let me try to remember . . . she said Tiffany was my half sister, but she got adopted by some people, the Twittys or something like that.

My mind goes blank. I'm so confused, I don't even take her hand and shake it.

"Sorry about that," she says, and gives me a sweet smile and a little giggle. "I get clumsy when I'm nervous."

She has a nice smile—I like it. It shows off her chubby red cheeks and big blue eyes. She looks like the kids you see in toothpaste commercials, smiling like they're really happy to be brushing their teeth fifty times a day. But she sure doesn't look anything like me!

"Your name is Dorinda?" Tiffany asks me, her eyes getting even wider.

"Yeah."

"I'm Tiffany."

"Hi," I reply, not knowing what else to say.

"This is so weird, huh?" Tiffany says. I can tell she's excited. And it doesn't seem to bother her at all that I'm black.

Mrs. Tattle must have told her about me. But when she told me about Tiffany, she never mentioned the fact that she's white.

Why not? I wonder. Is it because she thought I'd be prejudiced and wouldn't like her?

That's ridiculous, I think. I'm not prejudiced—I've never been prejudiced. I mean, I live with a bunch of kids that are white, black, red, and brown, and I love them all just the same. But how can my natural half sister be white? It just doesn't make any sense!

I'm waiting for Mrs. Tattle to explain, but she doesn't say boo—and Tiffany just keeps smiling at me, kinda like a friendly puppy, expecting me to say something more.

Finally, Mrs. Tattle gets up. She motions for us to walk with her. "Aren't you cold, Tiffany?"

"No, I'm all right."

I think Tiffany's shorts are too short, and maybe that's why her cheeks are so red. If Ms. Dorothea saw her in those white shorts after Labor Day, she'd get sent to Cheetah Girls detention for the rest of her life! White after

Labor Day is a fashion no-no! No way is she meeting my crew in *that* outfit!

"Dorinda, are you sure you don't want something to eat?" Mrs. Tattle asks me, like she wishes I would say yes.

"No, I'm fine." What I really want to say is, what in the world is going on here!

"Well, I know you two girls have a lot to talk about, so why don't we go sit on the bench?" Mrs. Tattle suggests. Then she quickly adds, "Or would you rather go skating first?"

"Skating," Tiffany says right away. She starts skating along, and I push off on my skateboard, keeping alongside of her. Tiffany looks over at me, like she's really happy to meet me. Obviously, she couldn't care less that I'm black.

She's really nice, I think. And just then, because she's not looking where she's going, she trips over a piece of garbage, starts wobbling, and falls flat on her butt!

Dang, she is clumsy! That is not at *all* like me!

"You okay, Tiffany?" Mrs. Tattle asks, helping her up.

I just stand there, too spaced out to realize I ought to help, too. I feel stupid about it, and guilty, too. I mean my reflexes are kinda in slow

Dorinda's Secret

71

motion, and my brain feels like a big blob of cotton candy. Tiffany said she gets clumsy when she's nervous. Maybe we aren't so different after all—just a different kind of clumsy.

"That's why I wear knee pads," Tiffany says apologetically. Then she sees my knees, which don't have pads on them, and I realize she knows why I don't have any safety equipment. "Oh. Sorry. That was a stupid thing to say."

"It's only cause my little brother lost them," I explain. *And because we're too poor to afford new equipment right away*, I add silently. "I usually wear all that stuff."

"I have an extra set of equipment at home," Tiffany says. "I'll bring it for you next time. You can keep it—I don't use it anymore."

Suddenly I feel bad, because I wasn't nice to Tiffany when Mrs. Tattle first introduced us. She sure is being nice to me.

"Your skates are dope," I say, warming up to her. I can tell they cost a lot of duckets; that's for sure. Her adoptive parents must be doing all right.

"Thanks," she giggles back. "How'd you learn how to skateboard?"

"When I was eight, I used to have this friend

named Sugar Bear. He taught me how to skate on his board 'cuz I used to help him with his homework. Then I got my own skateboard, last year."

"What happened to you and Sugar Bear— did you have a big fight or something? How come you're not still friends?"

"One night two years ago, his mother didn't come home. That's what my neighbor Ms. Keisha told me. Ms. Keisha knows everybody's business in Cornwall Projects. She knew I was tight with Sugar Bear. She told me he got sent down South to live with his grandmother."

I can feel my throat tighten up, remembering it. "He didn't even get to say good-bye to me."

"I'm sorry," Tiffany says. She means it, too, I can tell. Her eyes have tears in them, just as if it happened to her.

"I wanna learn how to ride a skateboard," Tiffany says, her eyes opening wide and getting twinkly. "Will you teach me sometime?"

"Okay," I say. "If you promise you won't skateboard right into a tree."

Tiffany laughs. "You must think I'm the clumsiest person on the whole planet," she says.

"You're all right," I say, and I mean it, too. It

doesn't matter to me that she's white. But I still can't believe we're sisters!

We stop in front of an old-looking park bench, and Mrs. Tattle catches up to us. "Let's sit right here," she says, motioning to Tiffany. Both of us sit down like robots, on either side of her. I can tell we're both more comfortable with each other when Mrs. Tattle isn't around.

"Tiffany, why don't you tell Dorinda a little about yourself?" Mrs. Tattle prods gently.

"You mean, about finding the records and stuff?" Tiffany asks, with a sly little smile on her face.

"Well, that's not *exactly* what I mean, but whatever you'd like to tell Dorinda would be fine," Mrs. Tattle counters, sounding like a principal.

"Oh, okay," Tiffany says. She giggles, then moves her feet in parallel motion, so her Rollerblades screech on the ground. I guess she's nervous.

"Well, I was looking through my parents' drawers—I was trying to find—I guess I had no business doing it, but I'm the curious type— nosy, you know? And sometimes I just can't help myself.

"Anyway, I came across this box, so I opened it. There was all sorts of baby stuff inside," Tiffany says, looking at me. "Baby booties, a little spoon, and some baby pictures. On the back of them it said, 'Karina, eleven months.'"

Her smile is gone now, as she remembers the moment she found the pictures. I can see the tears welling up in her eyes; and now I'm getting emotional, too—feeling it along with her.

"Then I found the adoption papers . . . and I saw the name Karina again, Karina Farber. It was next to *my* name—Tiffany Twitty. That's when I realized—*I* must be Karina Farber—the baby in the picture!"

"You mean, you didn't know you were adopted?" I blurt out.

"No!" Tiffany says, getting all emphatic like she's trying to avoid static. "I swear I didn't!"

"Don't swear, Tiffany," Mrs. Tattle says, flexing again on the principal tip. "Dorinda was just asking you a question. Some adoptive parents inform the adopted child when they're old enough to understand. Some choose not to."

"Well, my parents never told me *anything*," Tiffany says with an attitude. Then she gets quiet.

"Now, go on, Tiffany," Mrs. Tattle says, prodding her.

"So anyway, I started reading all the papers. There was a lot of stuff in there—like my real mother's and father's names—Eugene and Frances Farber!"

My mother's name was Frances Rogers. I've known that for years and years. I guess she took the name Farber when she hooked up with Tiffany's birth father.

I roll my foot on my skateboard, which is flat on the ground. I'm waiting to hear how she came to know about me.

"Then it said that my birth mother had a child from a previous marriage," Tiffany says. "It said she gave that child up, too. Just like she gave me up." She looks up at me and smiles. "So that's how I knew I had a sister."

Tiffany gets quiet again. Maybe my attitude is making her uncomfortable. I smile at her, to let her know it's okay with me that she's white.

Tiffany smiles back at me, and says, "By the way, your name was the same in the records— it's always been Dorinda. I guess that's because you weren't adopted or anything."

"Dorinda," Mrs. Tattle takes over. "Your

mother surrendered custody of both her children at the same time. You were eighteen months old, and Tiffany was seven months. You were placed in a foster home, and Tiffany was placed with adoptive parents."

"You're trying to tell me that Tiffany got adopted because she's white, and I didn't, because I'm black?"

Mrs. Tattle clears her throat. I can see this is difficult for her. "I'm sorry, Dorinda," she says. "The agencies tried to place both of you, but we were only able to place Tiffany. The caseworkers did the best they could."

Now I'm crying buckets. "That's so unfair!" I say through my tears.

Tiffany hugs me. She's crying, too. "I wish we could have stayed together," she says. "I've always missed having a sister."

I push her away, angry that no one wanted me. I'm sure it was because I'm black and Tiffany's white. Not that it's Tiffany's fault, but why can't people see that a black child is just as sweet and good as a white one?

"I still don't understand how Tiffany could be my sister," I blurt out. "She doesn't look half black. Is she?"

77

Mrs. Tattle gasps, surprised. "Dorinda," she says hesitantly, "you *do* know that your mother is *white*, don't you?"

"*No!*"

I can hear the words leave my mouth, but my mind sorta goes numb. I stare down at my sneakers, because I'm too embarrassed to look either Mrs. Tattle or Tiffany in the face. I feel stupid. "Nobody ever told me!" I moan.

I can't believe this! Here I am, wondering how Tiffany could possibly be my sister if she's not part black—and all the time, I'm half white!

Well, so what? I say to myself. Galleria's half white. Chanel's all kinds of things mixed up in one cute *cuchifrita*. I guess it's okay that I am what I am. I just can't believe I've lived all these years and never known! How could they not have told me any of this? It makes me so furious, I could scream!

Mrs. Tattle heaves a sigh, then talks quickly, like someone who is trying to cover her booty. "Dorinda, you have to understand—so many things get lost in translation when a child is placed in foster care. A caseworker enters a new situation, and there isn't always enough time to explain everything."

Yeah, well, I understand, all right. Nobody cares enough about me to tell me anything but lies—not even Mrs. Bosco! And how unfair is it that Tiffany got adopted when she was only a little baby, and I'm still in a foster home at twelve years old?

I sit there, crying and crying, and Mrs. Tattle gets really uncomfortable. I still can't look at her, but I feel her shifting her weight on the bench.

"So what happened to our mother?" I finally manage to ask through my stream of tears.

Tiffany looks at Mrs. Tattle with bated breath. She probably doesn't know where our mother is either. I guess *that* wasn't in the files—or Tiffany would have already told me the whole story.

"Well," Mrs. Tattle says, "according to the records, she went to California, and became involved in, um, some sort of social organization. But that was several years ago, and we've lost track of her since that time."

I secretly wonder if Mrs. Tattle is telling a fiberoni. Maybe she doesn't *want* to tell me—I mean—us, the truth. Tiffany looks at me as if she's thinking the same thing. What kind of organization is Mrs. Tattle talking about? Why doesn't she just come out and say it?

Instead of asking Mrs. Tattle, I turn to Tiffany. "How did you find me?"

"I told my parents I found the records," Tiffany says proudly. "Then I told them I wanted to meet my sister."

"You didn't get in trouble?" I ask, surprised.

"No way—they felt bad for not telling me everything in the first place," Tiffany explains, cracking that mischievous grin again.

I find myself smiling back. Tiffany is kinda funny. And she's got some serious mojo, too, to stand up to her parents like that!

"They know I'm here, and everything," she tells me. "They even wanted to come and meet you, but I told them, 'No way!'"

Now Mrs. Tattle is smiling too. "Tiffany's parents contacted us, and told us that Tiffany wanted to meet her sister. Then we contacted Mrs. Bosco. She gave her consent, as long as it was okay with you."

Now I feel bad that I got mad at Mrs. Bosco. She probably thought all this would be good for me. And I guess it *is*—except now I can feel this stabbing pain in my chest. It's this achy feeling, like my heart is broken. Somebody isn't telling the truth about something—*that's* what I'm talking about.

"Would you girls like to go skating together while I sit here?" Mrs. Tattle asks, concerned.

"Okay," I mumble, then get up and start dragging my back foot on the deck of my skateboard. Tiffany skates alongside me. "You don't look the way I imagined," she says smiling.

"Yeah, I guess not," I chuckle. I bet she didn't know I was black.

"No, I mean I thought you'd be chubby like me," Tiffany says, giggling.

"I'm getting skinnier, though," she goes on. "I've been on a diet. I already lost five pounds! Of course, I'll probably never be as thin as you."

That makes me chuckle. I can't imagine Tiffany without her cute, chubby cheeks. They kinda fit her. "It must be your dad's genes," I say.

"My dad's what?"

"Genes. You'll learn all about it in biology when you get to high school," I tell her.

Wait till Tiffany meets Ms. Dorothea, I say to myself with a smile. Then she won't worry about dieting anymore.

Suddenly, I shriek inside. Tiffany can't meet Ms. Dorothea—she can't meet my crew! No way, José—not yet, anyway! They wouldn't understand about me having a white sister. I had a hard enough time understanding it myself!

I look over at Tiffany, who is happily and clumsily skating along. "Did you just learn how to skate?" I ask.

"No. I've been skating for a long time," Tiffany says proudly.

I'm surprised. Maybe she doesn't have good coordination or something. Secretly, I can't help thinking, I don't believe she's my sister. We don't look alike, and she isn't anything like me.

Then the big bulb from above goes off in my head. Tomorrow I have biology. I'm gonna ask my teacher, Mr. Roundworm, about it. Maybe he can tell me if this whole thing is a hoax-arama.

"Where do you live?" Tiffany asks me.

"Harlem," I shoot back. "One-hundred-and-sixteenth Street."

"Oh," Tiffany says, kinda embarrassed.

"Where do you live?"

"Eighty-second Street and Park Avenue," she

says, then scrunches up her nose. "I hate it—I liked California better."

"You lived in California?" I ask curiously.

"Yeah, till I was seven."

"I can't believe you really found your adoption records like that!" I tell her.

"Actually, I found the locked security box, and then I searched all over the house until I found the key," Tiffany says proudly. "It took me two Saturday afternoons!"

I laugh out loud. It seems Tiffany's a whole lot better at sleuthing than skating.

"Where do you go to school?" I ask her.

"St. Agatha's of the Peril," Tiffany says, like she's disgusted. "I hate it. They're so strict there. Yesterday I had to go to detention, just because I was wearing nail polish. They made me take it off, too." She scrunches up her nose to show me she's unhappy. "Where do you go?"

"Fashion Industries East High," I say proudly.

"Wow, that is so cool!" Tiffany responds. "I love clothes but I'm tired of my mom picking out everything."

The way she looks at me, all impressed like

that, it makes me feel proud and excited about everything that I'm trying to do. So I tell her some more about myself.

"I design some stuff, too—and I'm in this singing group, the Cheetah Girls," I tell her.

"Yeah, Mrs. Tattle told me. I'm really into music. Maybe I could come hear you sing some time."

"Uh, yeah," I say, because I don't want to hurt her feelings. But inside, I'm saying, *I don't think so*. I can just see the looks on my crew's faces.

"I can tell Mrs. Tattle's really proud of you," Tiffany says.

I guess I never thought about it—but if it's true, I'm glad. "You don't have a caseworker, right?" I ask.

"No," Tiffany responds.

"Yeah, I guess not."

All of a sudden, Tiffany bumps into a garbage can and stumbles. We both start laughing. When she regains her balance, she moans, "I'm tired of skating—you?"

Even though I'm not, I say, "Let's go eat some hot dogs."

Tiffany smiles, and her eyes light up. She and

the twins would get along hunky chunky—the way they cook, Tiffany would probably never leave their house!

Whoa! There I go again, I think, and stop myself. The twins would not understand about Tiffany. And neither would the others.

"I wanna be a singer, too," Tiffany tells me, like it's a big secret.

As we skate back toward Mrs. Tattle, I tell Tiffany about everything that's happened so far with the Cheetah Girls. She seems really fascinated.

"I'm trying to get my parents to let me go to performing arts school," she says. "They want me to go to Catholic school," Tiffany informs me sadly. "We fight about it all the time." Then her big blue eyes light up. "You know, I just got a keyboard for my birthday!"

"That's dope," I exclaim. "I don't know how to play any instruments, even though I've always wanted to play the piano. See, Mrs. Bosco didn't have any money to get me lessons."

"Maybe you could come over my house and we could learn keyboard together!" Tiffany offers, getting excited.

I wonder why she's being so nice to me. She

doesn't even *know* me—and who says we're *really* sisters, huh? I'm still not totally convinced this isn't all some big mistake.

"Okay," I say, because I don't want to hurt Tiffany's feelings.

"My parents wanted to pick me up from the park," Tiffany says, grimacing. "They want to go with me *everywhere*."

I can tell something is wrong at home, but I don't say anything. Maybe Tiffany is just spoiled or something.

We finally get back to where Mrs. Tattle is sitting. She looks at Tiffany, then at me—so I smile to let her know everything is "hunky chunky."

"Well, I guess I'd better get you girls back home safely," Mrs. Tattle volunteers.

Tiffany turns to me. "Can I have your phone number?" she asks.

I hear myself saying "Okay," like I've been doing all afternoon. I scribble my phone number on a piece of paper and hand it to Tiffany.

"Can I have a hug?" she asks me, pushing away a blond curl that has fallen in her face. She really does remind me of Chanel. Too bad I can't introduce them. . . .

"Sure," I say, extending my arms and giving

her a hug. I feel her hair on the side of my face—it's really soft. She sorta feels like a little teddy bear. I can smell the soft scent of baby powder.

"I'm so glad I met you," Tiffany says, like she's just taken a trip to Treasure Island.

Suddenly, I feel myself fighting back tears again. I haven't cried this much since my almost-adoption party!

Chapter 7

Seeing my crew on Monday morning in school is like being in the Twilight Zone. I can't shake this whole thing about Tiffany, but I'm not talking about it with my crew—not yet. I know I'm kinda secretive, but that's me.

"Do' Re Mi, what you thinking without blinking?" Bubbles coos at me after first period.

"Nothing. I've just gotta roll into this biology class, and I haven't quite gotten this DNA thing down yet," I say, mustering up a pretty good half-true fib-eroni on the Q.T.—on the quick tip.

"Well, don't feel bad. I haven't done my Spanish homework either—*Yo no sé*, okay?"

That sends Chanel into the chuckles. "If you

would ask me, I would help you, Bubbles."

"I'll bet—then you'd be asking me to borrow duckets all the time, too. No way, José," Bubbles says, half-joking—but I know she means it.

Then she turns to me again. "So who did you meet yesterday, Do' Re Mi?"

"Oh, that didn't even come through," I lie, proud once again of my Q.T. handiwork. "Mrs. Tattle—my caseworker—just wanted to hang with me and some other kids, because she's going on vacation."

"What were they like?" Chanel asks curiously.

"Who?"

"The other kids."

"Oh, I don't know, Chanel—I don't want to talk about it," I sigh, because I can't tell one more fib-eroni. I guess I've filled my quota for one day, you know what I'm saying?

"Any word yet from the 'Battle of the Divettes' peeps?" I ask, changing the subject.

"Not yet," Bubbles says, heaving a sigh. "But my mom knows she'd better let us know the Minute Rice second she hears—she swore she'd call me on my cell phone!"

"See ya at lunch," I say, hugging both of them.

I feel relieved when I'm by myself again. I wish I never knew anything about foster care, or adoption, or any of this drama!

Sliding into my seat in biology class, I am on gene alert. I can feel my ears perk up when Mr. Roundworm mentions DNA.

"One of the most fascinating aspects of genetics is that an organism's DNA is more than a program for telling its cell how to operate. It is also an archive of the individual's evolutionary history." Mr. Roundworm taps a piece of chalk on the blackboard, next to the diagram he has drawn of a strand of DNA. It looks like pieces of ribbons wrapped together.

"If it were possible to align all the DNA strands of a baby in a single line, it would be long enough to make, on average, fifteen round trips from the sun to Pluto, the farthest planet in the solar system."

A trip around the world. That's it! I'd completely forgotten what my first foster mother, Mrs. Parkay, told me about my mom when I was little. She said my mother was on a trip around the world. Well, my mother must've had fifteen round trips from the sun to Pluto, too, because she has never come back!

When biology class is over, I can't wait to run up to Mr. Roundworm; but somebody else has beaten me to it. As usual, Albert Casserola has a question about our biology homework. Mr. Roundworm could repeat it fifty times, and Albert still wouldn't understand it.

Finally, Albert and his foggy glasses are out of my way. "Mr. Roundworm, can I talk to you for a second?" I ask politely.

"Yes, Dorinda," Mr. Roundworm responds, then waits for me to talk.

I look around to see who's listening, and Mr. Roundworm gets my drift.

"Let's go outside. We can talk while I'm walking to my office," he says, sticking a pen into the pocket of his lab coat.

"Um, I was wondering about this whole gene thing," I begin, struggling to find the right words. I mean, I still don't know how to ask my question without sounding stupid. "If a lady has a child with one man, then has a child with another man, can the two children look like they aren't related? I mean *really* not related?"

"Absolutely," Mr. Roundworm says, adjusting his thick-rimmed glasses.

I still don't feel satisfied with Mr. Roundworm's response, so I cut to the chase. "What I mean is, Mr. Roundworm, my mother was white—so is it possible for me to have a white sister—with blue eyes and blond hair?"

"Okay, I see what your question is. This lady—your mother—has a child with an African American, and that child is you."

"Right," I respond.

"Then she has a child with a Caucasian male. What you're asking me is would this other child look Caucasian?"

"Yes," I say, feeling stupid now for real. I hate that term—"African American." It makes me uncomfortable, and it sounds like I don't really belong here or something.

"Yes, she would—and I can tell you something even more interesting," Mr. Roundworm says, smiling at me in an understanding way. "Since you have a white mother, *you* may have recessive genes for blond hair and blue eyes. That means if you had a child with a man that has blond hair and blue eyes, *you* could give birth to a child with blond hair and blue eyes."

"Word?" I say, ruminating on the situation.

"Genes are amazing things—and they have a mind of their own," Mr. Roundworm says, beaming at me.

"Yeah, I guess so," I respond, trying to appear as enthusiastic as Mr. Roundworm. He is definitely a cool teacher—at least I never fall asleep in his class.

"Good-bye, Dorinda. I hope I've helped you," Mr. Roundworm says, looking concerned.

"Good-bye, Mr. Roundworm."

After he leaves, I walk along the hallway in a daze. I feel like I'm in the Twilight Zone again. I'm so lost in my own world, I walk right into someone.

"Excuse me," I say apologetically.

The girl just smiles, nasty-like, and walks away. Sometimes I think I have a case of fleas, please, the way some peeps catch an attitude for no reason.

I still can't believe Tiffany is really my sister. If my mom was here, she could tell me. Feeling the tears well up in my eyes, I make myself snap out of it. I have to go to draping class now, and I don't want to start thinking about my mother, or I'll start crying all over the stupid muslin!

Draping class winds up being the best therapy I could have had. I get busy working on ideas for Cheetah Girls costumes, and by the time class is over, I've forgotten all about Tiffany and my mother.

I meet my crew for lunch, and that's when Galleria pounces.

"Yo, Do' Re Mi, weeza in the house, pleeza, weeza!" she exclaims, hugging me and jumping up and down. I wait for Galleria to stop, so she can tell me why she's so amped. Only this morning, she looked like she needed fifty cups of mochaccino (her favorite Italian coffee) to get her flow going—you know what I'm saying?

"We got into the competition!" she yells, and then starts taking deep breaths to calm down.

"Word!" I say, bugging my eyes, 'cuz now I'm getting amped, too!

Chanel comes outside to meet us, and Galleria puts on the same cheetah-certified show. "*Hola*, granola! Weeza in the house, weeza in the house!"

Chuchie starts jumping up and down, screaming. She doesn't even ask what Galleria is talking about. Sometimes the two of them communicate without saying a word, you know what I'm saying?

Even though I'm happy, I feel that stabbing pain in my chest again—you know, kinda like my heart is cracked in pieces. Those two are bound till death, the dynamic duo, yo. They're just letting me be part of *their* crew. They're more like sisters than any sister I'll ever have, I bet.

All of a sudden, Chanel starts hugging me too. Whew. That makes me feel a little better, like I'm part of our crew after all. I take a deep breath, and wait for Galleria to give us the details about next Saturday.

"It's a good thing we just performed in the New Talent Showcase," Galleria says excitedly, " 'cuz we are definitely ready to battle with Freddy—"

"Or any divette with a microphone—'cuz when we 'rock it to the beat, it's rocked to the doggy bone,' " Chanel joins in, singing the lyrics from Galleria's song "Woof, There It Is." I join in for a chorus, as we walk to Mo' Betta Burger on Eighth Avenue to get our grub on.

When we get there, Galleria fills us in on the "Divette" scoop. "We have a microphone check at three o'clock Saturday and the doors open at seven P.M."

"Are the divettes representing from other places?" I ask, curious. See, when we performed in Def Duck Records' New Talent Showcase in Los Angeles, they had groups from all over the country.

"No doubt about the East Coast clout," Galleria says, nodding her head. "This is a regional contest, but the competition finals are gonna be held in the Big Apple, too, you know what I'm saying? Because they're not playing—they know the winner is probably gonna come from the East Coast."

Galleria bops along with a satisfied smirk. She is so sure that we are gonna blow up our spots. "We have to be there at six sharp for the performance."

"We'll be there or be T-square," I say, bopping along, too.

"What are we gonna sing?" Chuchie asks.

Oh, no, I think. Here we go again, with the drama over who gets to write our songs.

"Why, Chuchie?" Bubbles asks. "Have you written one we should memorize overnight and perform on Saturday, *so we can lose the competition*?" Like I said, these two are like sisters, Galleria can tell when Chanel has a few hedgehog tricks up her sleeve.

"What happened?" Chanel exclaims, like she always does when she gets flustered. "No, I haven't written any songs, *babosa*, but I thought maybe we could sing the one we wrote together—'It's Raining Benjamins.'"

Actually, Galleria told me that Chanel only wrote one line in the whole song, but I can't blame Chanel for trying. She just wants to feel like she has "Big Willy" skills too.

"Chuchie, we *are* going to perform 'It's Raining Benjamins'—but not on Saturday. We need more time to practice it and work out a routine or something." Galleria crosses her arms in front of her, like that's the end of the conversation.

The big bulb from above goes off in my head again. "Yo, check it, remember what Aqua said? Maybe we should throw money on the stage for 'It's Raining Benjamins'—like the Cash Money Girls did at the New Talent Showcase," I suggest. "We could come up with some dope choreography and everything, right?"

"Do' Re Mi has a point. That sounds like the joint," Galleria says, looking at Chanel like, "Give it up, *mamacita*."

"*Está bien,*" Chanel says, twirling her hair, then breaking out in a mischievous grin. "You're right. We should wait."

That grin reminds me of Tiffany. It's the same exact look! I'm about to burst out laughing. But then, the chill comes back, and I force myself to get my mind on the game plan at hand.

Galleria hugs Chanel, and I can see they have squashed their beef jerky for now. Then Galleria lets out a rally like she's in Cali: "We're not having a 'Nightmare on 125th Street' again —this time, we're bringing the noise, 'cuz we're poised!"

Chapter 8

When I get home, Mrs. Bosco tells me that Tiffany phoned and asked for me. "Dorinda, what's the matter, baby? You didn't like her?" Mrs. Bosco asks, because she sees the troubled look on my face.

"No, she was nice," I reply. I don't want to bad-mouth Tiffany for no reason. She *is* nice, and I feel sorry for her, 'cuz she *needs* a big sister or something. I could tell that she was kinda lonely. "I just feel strange about the whole situation."

What I don't want to tell Mrs. Bosco is the truth—that I'm mad at her. I know it's not all her fault—she can't read or write, so she probably doesn't know what's in my records—but

I *feel* like it's her fault anyway.

"Mrs. Tattle says my mother is white," I blurt out.

"I guess so," Mrs. Bosco says. I try to figure out if that means she didn't know, or that she can't believe it—like me.

Mrs. Bosco starts coughing—*badly*. I get scared that she's getting sick again. She was hospitalized for acute bronchitis last summer, and she hasn't really recovered from it. I don't want to get her upset now or anything.

She sits down on the couch in the living room, keeping the tissue held up to her mouth. "You know, it wouldn't hurt you to spend some time with that child," she says, talking through the tissue.

"Okay," I say. "But I can't this week. I have rehearsals every day for the competition on Saturday."

"You got another show?" she asks, her eyes getting brighter.

"Yes," I say, smiling because I'm so excited about it. At least the Cheetah Girls are still in the running, in more ways than one, you know what I'm saying? "It's called 'Battle of the Divettes' competition," I explain.

That makes Mrs. Bosco chuckle, and that makes her start coughing again. I decide to shut up, but she keeps egging me on. "Where's it gonna be?" she asks.

"It's at the Apollo Theatre," I say, and then wait for her response. Mrs. Bosco felt so bad for me when the Cheetah Girls lost the Amateur Hour contest.

"Never mind what happened last time," she says, reading my mind again. "Remember what I told you then—one monkey don't stop no show."

I smile, because I know how she loves me. I just hope she doesn't get sick. If I ever lost Mrs. Bosco, I don't know what I would do—not to mention all the other foster kids in our house.

"They ain't gonna have that Sandman fool onstage again," Mrs. Bosco says, her eyes twinkling. The Sandman is the one who pulls groups offstage when the Amateur Hour crowd boos them.

"No, I don't think so," I tell her. "But they are gonna have a lot of judges."

"Lord, I don't know which is worse," Mrs. Bosco says, wanting to laugh but not daring to 'cuz she might start coughing again.

"The winner of the competition gets to compete in the finals, then *that* winner gets to appear on the television show *The Grade*," I say, talking slowly so she can follow what I'm saying.

Mrs. Bosco nods her head. "They sure make you dance around like a monkey with a tin cup full of pennies before they give you anything, huh?"

Now it's my turn to laugh. "Yeah, I guess so."

"I left that child's number on a piece of paper in the kitchen," Mrs. Bosco says, looking at me like she wants me to call Tiffany.

"Okay. Um, I'll get it later," I say, to avoid talking about it anymore. "I have to go down to Chanel's house now for rehearsal." I get out of that room before she starts in on me to call Tiffany.

I'm in my bedroom, getting everything I need to go downtown with, and I'm thinking things over. I wonder why Tiffany called me. Maybe she wants to be like real sisters, calling each other all the time, getting all involved with each other's lives.

Well, that may be fine for her, but I don't

know if I'm really ready to let a new sister into my life. I've already got all these kids in the house with me who I love, and take care of. And I've got my crew—which brings me to the other thing. How are they gonna react when they hear I have a white sister? Would they accept her if she started hanging around with us?

See, Galleria's an only child, Aqua and Angie don't have any other brothers and sisters, and Chanel's only got her little brother Pucci, who just turned nine. It would be way different if Tiffany were there at our rehearsals—she's almost my age!

Which is another thing—Tiffany knows how old I really am! What if she told my crew? Would they still even want to be friends with me, let alone let me stay in The Cheetah Girls?

And what if Tiffany decides she wants to be *part* of the group? I don't think my crew is gonna be down with taking on any new members, let alone Tiffany!

So I'm standing there, fretting about all this stuff, when Twinkie runs over and hands me a cookie. "Thank you," I say, giving her a big hug.

"Can I come with you?" she pleads.

"It's just a boring old rehearsal," I say, so she won't feel bad. "Guess what—when I come home later, we are gonna do our own Cheetah Girls rehearsal! Would you like that?"

"Yeah!"

I hug Twinkie again. One day, I want her and all my brothers and sisters to come to a big stadium, sit in the front row, and watch The Cheetah Girls perform. But not yet—not while we're still divettes!

When I walk into Chanel's house, her little brother, Pucci, practically grabs my arm out of its socket. "You gotta see Mr. Cuckoo!" he exclaims.

Pucci is so cute—he's got that big gap in between his two front teeth, and the Cupid's bow on his upper lip—and that same jumping-bean energy like Chanel. You can't help smiling at him all the time.

"Come on, I'll show you," he says, dragging me into his bedroom, which is inhabited by a tribe of Whacky Babies stuffed animals, who look like they're ready to pounce off the shelves!

"*There* he is!" Pucci says, pointing to the cage in the corner of his room, where I see the African pygmy hedgehog I helped Chanel pick out at the exotic pet store for Pucci's birthday.

I bend down to check out Mr. Cuckoo. "Wow, Pucci, you hooked him up—Cuckoo is definitely chillin' in his new crib!"

Pucci grins. I see a book peeking out from under the bedspread on his bed. Dragging it on the floor, I read the title: *Harry Henpecker's Guide to Geography*. It's the book Pucci's father gave him for his birthday. I flip through the pages and look at all the places around the world I wanna see.

"You can have it if you want it," Pucci offers.

"No, that's all right," I respond. I feel bad for him. I know what it's like to get presents you don't want. When I first got to Mrs. Bosco's, Mrs. Parkay sent me a present on Christmas. It was some stupid stuffed giraffe, and I threw it in the corner behind the Christmas tree, because I didn't want anything from her. Besides, what I really wanted was a doll wearing pretty clothes.

The doorbell rings, and I hear Aqua's and

Angie's voices cackling away. "I gotta go, Pucci, we have rehearsal now."

"You gonna go to the Apollo again, right?" Pucci asks.

"Yeah."

"How come they let you back in there, if you already lost?" he asks, his eyes opening wide. I chuckle, realizing he doesn't understand.

"That was the Amateur Hour contest we lost, Pucci," I say. "Now we're gonna perform in the 'Battle of the Divettes' competition. It just happens to be at the same place, but it has nothing to do with the Apollo—you understand?"

"Oh," Pucci says, fiddling with his computer. "You gonna have Cheetah Boys now? Can I be in the group?" Pucci flashes his mischievous grin so I know he's angling for a dangle—a cheesing skill he learned from his older sister, no doubt.

That's all we need. Pucci in the group, with Tiffany, too—and throw in Twinkie for good measure. "Who knows?" I joke to Pucci. "Maybe Cuckoo will come onstage and perform with us, too—you know what I'm saying?"

"Yeah, right," Pucci says, smirking.

"I'm not playing, you know what I'm saying?"

I hear Chanel calling me, so I run to the exercise studio, where we usually rehearse.

"Hi Aqua. Hi, Angie," I say, hugging the twins. I don't get to see them as much as I see Chanel and Galleria, since we don't go to the same school. They're all wrapped up in talking about going home to Houston for Thanksgiving. I can definitely tell they're excited about it.

"I wish Daddy was coming with us, though," Angie says, kinda sad. "We're scared to leave him here with that High Priestess girlfriend of his."

"I know that's right," I chime in. I met their father's girlfriend, High Priestess Abala Shaballa, and she does seem to be tripping in another galaxy, if you know what I'm saying.

"There's plenty of time to worry about looking good in the 'hood, Miz Aquanette," Galleria says cheerfully, tapping her foot like she's ready to get down to the business at hand. "'There's always a new day in the jiggy jungle,'" she starts singing, "'so let's not bungle our chance to rise for the prize, and show you who we are, in the jiggy jiggy jungle—'"

We all sing along, since that's what we're here for—rehearsing our act, you know what I'm saying?

I'm so tired by the time I get home from Chanel's house that I head straight to my bedroom. Today's rehearsal was exhausting—not only running through all our songs and dance routines, but having to keep my mind off everything that's happening in my personal life. I'll tell you, if I didn't have Saturday's competition to think about, I'd be going loony right about now.

Just as I flop down on my bed, I hear Mrs. Bosco calling my name from her bedroom. "I'll be right there," I yell. Getting back up, I poke my head into Mrs. Bosco's bedroom.

"Dorinda—that child called *again* while you were out."

"Tiffany?" I ask, sighing, but what I'm really thinking is, Doesn't she have anything better to do than bother me?

"Thanks, Mom," I say, hoping she'll squash this conversation, but I shoulda known better.

"We had a nice long talk, you know," Mrs.

Bosco continues. She is propped up on the bed eating a bowl of rice pudding. "I think that child needs someone to talk to."

"Yeah," I say, nodding my head.

"She says her parents want to meet you 'cuz she can't stop talking about you," Mrs. Bosco says, beaming.

Oh, swelly, just what I need. Not just a new sister, but her parents, too!

"Maybe it's something important she needs to talk to you about," Mrs. Bosco suggests. "I think you better call her."

"After we do the competition," I say quickly. What I really mean is, after I've had time to break the news to my crew. "Then I'll go see Tiffany and her family," I offer, and quickly move on, changing the subject. "We had a great rehearsal tonight."

"That's good."

"I think we could really win this competition," I say—and for a change, I really mean it. I hope Mrs. Bosco doesn't ask to come to the competition, though, because I'm not ready to perform in front of her. I don't really want any of my family around until I feel ready for the big time, know what I'm sayin'?

"Good night," I say, stifling a yawn. Mrs. Bosco doesn't like to kiss or anything—I guess she doesn't want to get too close to us, in case we get taken away someday—so I just smile and walk out of her bedroom and back to my own.

Lying on my pillow, I wonder what Mrs. Bosco and Tiffany talked about. Tiffany Twitty sure gets chatty with everybody. I mean, she really runs her mouth faster than the Road Runner clocks miles.

I wonder if she looks like our mother . . . ?

Chapter 9

No matter how many times the Cheetah Girls perform, I always get a case of the spookies beforehand. Okay, so we haven't performed that much, but I'll bet it never goes away. Today is no exception. Even Aqua and Angie are faking that they're not quaking.

"Where's the Sandman?" Aqua asks, popping her eyes as she nervously looks around for him. Not that he booted us off the stage at the Amateur Hour contest—we came in second—but still, he's a scary somebody to think about when you're about to perform at the Apollo Theatre!

We are instructed to head backstage and see the competition coordinator. On our way down the aisle, I check out the big sparkly banner that is spanning the stage: HOT 99 PRESENTS "THE BATTLE OF THE DIVETTES" COMPETITION.

Ms. Dorothea, who as our manager goes everywhere with us, is wearing a cheetah-spotted bustier, and her chest is covered with glitter. She looks like a movie star or something. One of the stagehands is goo-gahhing and peering down at Ms. Dorothea from the top of his ladder.

"If he paid as much attention to his job as he does to me, this place wouldn't be falling apart!" she humphs as she herds us around her.

The other stagehands are busy putting up banners. It seems like there are lots of companies sponsoring the competition.

"Ooh, looky, cooky, S.N.A.P.S. Cosmetics is one of the sponsors," Galleria tells us, pointing to a banner.

A pretty girl with a Dr. Seuss–type hat and a clipboard is talking into a walkie-talkie. Then, spotting Ms. Dorothea, she calls out our group's name and walks over to us. "Well, I guess I had no trouble figuring out who you are," the Dr. Seuss lady says to Ms. Dorothea.

Ms. Dorothea beams, then says, "I'm Dorothea

Garibaldi, the manager of the Cheetah Girls."

"Omigosh, I thought you were part of the group!" the Dr. Seuss lady exclaims. "Well, you look *fabulous*—I love that bustier. Where did you get it?"

Ms. Dorothea goes on to tell the Dr. Seuss lady all about her boutique, Toto in New York . . . Fun in Diva Sizes. I can tell the Dr. Seuss lady is supa-dupa impressed.

"Oh, too bad I'm not big enough to shop there," she whines, like she really means it.

"Size is just an attitude, darling," Ms. Dorothea quips. "You're welcome to stop in any time."

"Thank you!" the lady gushes. Then she gets down to the business at hand—trying to organize the lineup of struggling divettes. "I'm Candy Kane, the Talent Panel Coordinator, and I'll tell you how everything works. Let's see . . ." she goes on, peering down at her clipboard. "The Cheetah Girls are number seven in the lineup."

"Sounds sweet to me, Miss Candy Kane," Ms. Dorothea responds. "How many groups are performing?"

"Um, let's see—seven."

"Oh, so we're last!" Ms. Dorothea says, her eyes brightening.

"Yes, I guess so," Candy Kane giggles.

"Are all the groups from New York?" Galleria asks nervously.

"I believe they are—since this is a regional contest."

"How many contests are there?" Ms. Dorothea asks.

"There are quite a few, but the finals are going to be held in New York City, you'll be happy to know."

Candy Kane winks at Galleria. I can tell she likes our groove. "Now here are the rules: You may wait in your dressing room if you like, or you may wait backstage. It's your responsibility to be backstage and standing under the green light in time for your performance."

Pointing upward to the green light, Candy continues, "You are not allowed to take pictures or use recording devices backstage. You are also not allowed to drink, eat, or smoke. After you finish your performance, you should exit the stage *quickly*, then wait back here for the announcer to give you your return cue— that is, *if* you become one of the finalists."

"Return cue—is that when the audience picks the winners?" Ms. Dorothea asks.

"No, Mrs. Garibaldi, the panel of judges seated in the first row is solely responsible for picking the finalists. The announcer will be handed three envelopes, and read the winners for the first and second runner-ups, as well as the regional winner. Only if your name is announced should you come back onstage. Do you understand everything?"

"Yes!" we say in unison.

Handing Ms. Dorothea some papers, Candy Kane explains, "Now here are the releases for you to sign. It's a standard release—stating that you're aware this event is being videotaped, and that you've not been promised any monetary compensation from Looking Good Productions for participating in the 'Battle of the Divettes' competition."

Ms. Dorothea puts on her cheetah glasses and scans the forms.

"When you're done, you can hand the forms to any of the production assistants back-stage—oh, and here are your gift bag tickets. I'll give you six—one for you, too, Mrs. Garibaldi. Just give them to Gator, the guy in the blue baseball cap standing right over there."

"I see him. And thank you!" Ms. Dorothea says, spotting the guy.

"He'll give you your gift bag, girls—you're gonna love all the goodies from our sponsors. And good luck!" Candy Kane whisks off to do her supa-spiel with the next divette-in-waiting, leaving us all hyped about this whole thing.

"The peeps doing this competition are definitely more chili than the Amateur Hour people," Galleria says, impressed. Then she turns to Chanel. "You sure perked up as soon as you heard there were free goodies," Galleria chides her.

Chanel breaks out in a mischievous grin. I love her so much—she makes everybody feel better with her *señorita* energy. For the moment, I've forgotten all my troubles—even my nerves are gone!

We hightail it over to Gator to get our gift bags. "See you later, Gator," Galleria says sweetly, as he hands us our last bag.

"Ooh, it's heavy," Chanel says excitedly, as she swings her red canvas McDonald's bag back and forth.

"They wouldn't put food in this thing, would they?" Aqua asks hopefully, as she gingerly puts her hand inside.

"No, silly, willy! McDonald's is obviously just one of the sponsors," Galleria mumbles. "Oh—S.N.A.P.S.!" she exclaims, taking a free lipstick sample out of her bag.

"Ooh, what color is it?" I ask, waiting for Galleria to take the top off and swivel up the lipstick. It turns out to be a red shade.

Galleria looks at the bottom of the tube to check out the name of the color. "'Desire.'"

Chanel has taken hers out, and giggles, "Mine is 'Destiny'"—but I don't like the color." I have to agree with her—it *is* a wack shade of yellow.

The twins have dug the tubes of lipstick out of their gift bags—naturally, they get the same color. "'Lust'?" Aqua moans when she reads the label. "We better not even take this home, or Daddy won't let us out of the house again!"

The twins' father, Mr. Walker, *is* kinda strict, so I decide to help them out. "I'll switch with you," I say. "I got a tube of 'Destiny,' too."

"I don't want that—our lips are big enough without looking like banana peels!" Aqua moans.

"Well, Aqua, you can either meet your 'Destiny' by getting shipped back to your Grandma's in Houston, or you can wear it," I chuckle, like a game show host. *"The choice is yours."*

"Awright," she mumbles, swiping my tube, and handing over hers. I can't believe how many goodies are stuffed in these bags! Little bottles of shampoo, pencils, an ugly paper-weight, a *Sistarella* magazine, Miss Wiggy glitter lip gloss, and sheets of butterfly stickers.

"Ooo, I can give these to my sister Twinkie!" I exclaim.

"Hey, Do' Re Mi—how come you never invite your family to come see you perform?" Chanel asks me sweetly.

My breath catches in my throat. Suddenly, my nerves are all back, and I can feel my stomach jumping. "I'm just not ready," I mumble, looking away.

"Yeah, I know what you mean. I sure wish Mom wasn't coming tonight," Chanel laments. "And guess what else—she's bringing her boyfriend with her—Mr. Tycoon himself! I'm not feeling in the mood for him, *está bien?*"

I feel so relieved that none of my "family"

will be in the house, because I don't know if I'm ready for that yet. Performing is scary enough without more drama. I'm afraid that if anybody I knew was out there in the audience, I'd just freeze up totally right there on stage.

I look up, wondering if Chanel has sensed how scared I am. But no, I have nothing to worry about—her greedy little paws are already digging into her bag, looking for treasures.

A little while later, after we've finished switching our Astrology bottles of cologne (Inside of my bag is a bottle of "Virgo," so I give it to the twins, since that's their astrological sign), we decide it's time to check out the talent. Galleria, Chanel, and I don't recognize any of the other girls hanging out in the backstage area with us. But the twins do.

"There's that girl JuJu from school," Angie winces to Aqua.

"Her name is JuJu 'Beans' Gonzalez," Angie explains to the rest of us, sucking her teeth. "She's a singing *and* drama major—with emphasis on the drama, you know what I'm sayin'?"

"Yeah—and her middle name describes her

exactly, 'cuz she iz 'full of beans!'" Aqua adds, poking out her juicy lips for extra measure.

By this time, JuJu "Beans" Gonzalez has gotten the drift that all eyes are on her. She looks over in our direction, then turns away as if she doesn't see us.

"I wonder how she got in this competition, 'cuz I didn't see any notice at school," Aqua ponders.

"The world of divettes is very small," Galleria offers in explanation. "Everything that's going down sure gets passed around."

"Yeah, well the world sure ain't big enough for us and JuJu!" Aqua laments, sucking on her lollipop. "She looks like one of those beauty pageant contestants back home in that outfit. Ain't that right, Angie?"

"Yes, ma'am," Angie agrees. "And we sure got a lot of girls who look like her back home."

I take in JuJu's red sequin gown, and the fake red gardenia flowers pinned in her upswept 'do, and decide "I think she looks like the runner-up for Miss Botanical Gardens!"

We all giggle, which helps us forget how nervous we are.

A woman in a red sweat suit and baseball

cap is walking around introducing herself to all the contestants. Now she comes up to us.

"Hi, I'm P.J. Powers from HOT 99," she says in a bubble-licious way, extending her hand to Galleria.

We all get instantly excited because we have just met P.J. Powers—the radio deejay on "The Power Hour," which plays the most flava-fied songs in heavy rotation. After she's shaken all our hands, she moves on to greet the next group.

Ms. Dorothea, meanwhile, has signed all the papers. "I guess it's time to pounce, girls. Let's go on up to the dressing room, so you can put on your costumes." She herds us toward the back stairway, which we remember from the Amateur Hour.

"Now we gotta go climb those creaky stairs into the tower of the haunted house," jokes Aqua. "I sure hope *this* horror show has a happy ending!"

Chapter 10

We decide to wait backstage rather than in our dressing room, because it's seven o'clock—and that means, "Show time at the Apollo!" Sometimes shows don't start on time, but you never know—and half the fun of performing with competing acts is hearing them do their thing, you know what I'm saying?

"Should we leave our gift bags in the dressing room?" Aqua asks Ms. Dorothea.

"No way, darling," she replies. "Why should one of these desperate divettes get their grubby little paws on our products?" Ms. Dorothea huffs then gathers up all six of the gift bags and puts them in her big cheetah carry-all. She always has a lot of papers and folders to carry, so she carries these really big bags.

All of a sudden the chatter in the audience dies down. Then they begin to clap loudly, which means the announcer has hit the stage. "How y'all doing tonight, Big Apple?!" P.J. Powers bellows into her microphone. Then she lets out a raucous chant: "Y'all are on HOT 99—so it's your dime!"

"Oh, that's *la dopa*! They're broadcasting the show *live* on the radio," Chanel says, jumping up and down.

Suddenly, I get the squigglies in my stomach again. Wow—this is really it! I grab Chanel's hand. Please don't let us lose, I pray. Not at the Apollo. Not again. Not live on the air!

"We've got prizes for you people!" P.J. Powers screams into the microphone, hyping the crowd. "So keep those ticket stubs. Because at some point during the show, we're going to be calling out winning numbers, to give back what you give me everyday on HOT 99—the flava, baybee!"

The crowd is cheering wildly.

"How many of y'all want to win a trip to the Bahamas, courtesy of HOT 99? That's right, you know what they say—it's betta in the

Bahamas! So you'd better stay in your seats, or you might miss out—you know what I'm saying?—'cuz P.J. Powers ain't *playing*!"

The curtain backstage is too thick to let us get a peek at anybody in the audience. "That's just as well," Angie offers as consolation. "The less we know the better."

"I just wonder who the judges are," I whisper.

Angie is wiping her forehead with a tissue. The twins sweat when they get nervous. They are *deathly* afraid of heights, and you should see them sweat whenever they ride an elevator above the tenth floor!

The first divette to perform is called Witch Hazel. What a name! I can't see her through the curtain, but I'll bet she comes onstage with a broom or something. I hear her drop an R & B song, which was originally sung by Diamonds in the Ruf. It's called "Bewitched."

I hate when acts perform covers of other artist's songs. It's like, "Can't you write your own music?"

We just look at each other and smile, and I know what we're all thinking: Witch Hazel better be putting a spell on the audience, because the hardest spot in a showcase is the first.

"Better her than us," Angie whispers in my ear. Witch Hazel gets a nice round of applause. That makes us feel a whole lot better—knowing that the audience will probably be all warmed up by the time we perform.

The next few singers also sing R & B tunes, but they aren't that good—except for the Butta Cups. They have a nice three-part harmony.

"I think the Cheetah Girls have got this one in the bag, baby," Galleria says, crossing her fingers because it's getting closer to our turn.

P.J. Powers announces Fakie Quakie, and two short girls in black vinyl miniskirts go running onto the stage. They start singing a song that sounds sorta gospel-ish. "'Since you left me/My heart's so achy. I'm not fakin' that I'm just quakin' . . . .'"

Aqua and Angie start bouncing around, because they *love* gospel music. And I've gotta admit these Fakie Quakie girls have nice soprano range. Better than mine, that's for sure. If I go too high up, my voice gets squeaky. It's better if I stay in the middle—that's what Drinka Champagne says.

The Cheetah Girls

It's time to do our Cheetah Girls prayer, so we gather in a circle and join hands. At the end of each prayer, we always end with our Cheetah Girls oath:

"We're the Cheetah Girls and we number five.
What we do is more than live.
We'll stay together through the thin and the thick.
Whoever tries to leave, gets hit with a chopstick.
Whatever makes us clever—forever!!!"

P.J. Powers *finally* announces us. We take a deep breath together, and run onstage. When we get there, the cheering drowns out everything else.

I try not to look for the video camera that is taping the competition, but I can't help sneaking a peek as we wait for our taped track to kick in. I don't see the camera, though—that must mean it's far in back of the house.

I notice that the Klieg lights are *really* bright this time. I liked the way they did the lighting for us at the New Talent Showcase in L.A. This is definitely way too bright. Oh, well, part of performing is just acting like everything is supa-dupa chili, so that's what I do as we dive into the song.

Is it me, or is the tape-recorded track louder than usual? There must be an echo in this place, or maybe it's haunted. I try to remember if I noticed that the last time we performed here, but I can't remember.

As we sing, I notice that it's taking us a while to really get into our flow, you know what I'm saying? Maybe it's the lights being so bright, or the track being so loud—or maybe it's just that we're goin' out live on the radio. Anyway, by the time we get to the third verse, we've got it all together, and we're rockin' the house:

"Some people move like snakes in the grass
or gorillas in the mist
who wanna get dissed.

Some people dance with the wolves
or trot with the fox
right out of the box."

When the five of us hold hands and take our bow, I feel how clammy Chanel's hand is. Or maybe it's my hand! I'm sweating a lot, and I didn't even notice it till now.

Right before we exit the stage, we cup our hands like cheetahs to make our "growl power" sign, then scrunch up our faces like we're gonna pounce. I hear a few people laughing in the audience, and the applause gets louder. Everybody loves that "growl power" thing—it's kinda cute, I guess.

Backstage, as we wait for the winners to be announced, the tension is so thick you could cut it with a knife. After all, this is it: do-or-die time. As far as I'm concerned, it's first place or nothing—I mean, who wants to be a runner-up every time, you know what I'm saying?

Chanel is clutching my hand really hard.

"All right y'all," P.J. Powers announces. "This is the moment we've all been waiting for. It's time to do *battle*! Which one of these divettes is gonna make it to the finals?" The audience whoops and shouts, calling out the names of different groups—including ours.

"Let me tell you something, I know those divettes are backstage quaking in their weaves," P.J. continues. "You know why? Well, lemme tell you in case you don't know. One *very, very* lucky and plucky divette act—that's unsigned talent, y'all, in case you don't know—is gonna make *The Grade* and compete on MTV!"

The crowd lets out another hoot.

"That's right, y'all. MTV will finance and air a professionally produced video of the grand prize winner! Now that winner could be one of these fierce divettes you just saw perform. Now what else we got?"

"What?" yells someone in the audience.

"We got *two* other hot spots—that's right, y'all, *two* other *lucky, lucky, lucky* divettes are gonna be our first and second runner-ups. Now they're not going to get to go to the finals—"

"Awwww," moans the audience.

"I know—life in the fast lane can be a pain, baby, *but* the first runner-up receives a cash prize! That's right—who doesn't like a little loot? Lemme hear ya if you would say no to a Benjamin knocking on your door! Lemme hear ya!"

There is one second of silence.

"That's what I thought," P.J. Powers continues, which wins a raucous laugh from the crowd. "The first runner-up will win a five-hundred-dollar cash prize—that's enough money for a new weave, right? Am I right, ladies?"

More laughter. Chanel is holding my hand so tight it's cutting off my circulation. I yank my hand away from her, and she giggles, then quickly covers her mouth when Galleria shoots her a look.

"The second runner-up? Well, we can't dis the second runner-up, can we? They're gonna get a guest deejay spot on my show—that's right, hanging on "The Power Hour" with the P.J. till payday! *And*, they will receive two back-stage passes to MTV's *The Hookup*,' to hang with today's hottest groups in the green room! Now that's the way I like to eat ribs, what about y'all?"

The crowd is cheering again. Galleria shoots me a look like, "Would she shut her trap, pleez, or we're gonna sneeze!"

"Okay, by the way, y'all, have you met our illustrious panel of judges? In the house with us tonight is everybody's favorite gossip diva—Miss Clucky!"

After the round of applause, P.J. introduces eight more judges, including "Miss Lela Lopez from *Sistarella* magazine, and Destiny

Davenport, Corporate Sponsorship Executive from S.N.A.P.S. Cosmetics."

I look at my crew. I guess we know where the name of that wack lipstick "Destiny" came from!

The squigglies start in my stomach again. If the Cheetah Girls weren't already quaking in our boots, we sure are now that we know who the judges are!

"Now for the moment we've all been waiting for. Miss Clucky, the envelope, please," P.J. Powers says, her voice tingling with excitement.

All five of us grab each other's hands as a drum roll sounds.

"Our *second* runner-up is—the Butta Cups! Give them a hand, people!"

We breath a sigh of relief. At least we aren't second runners-up!

When the Butta Cups hit the stage, P.J. Powers asks the audience, "Aren't they dainty little divettes? I love those cute little gloves. Do you eat ribs with them on?"

"No," says one of them into the microphone.

"Well, you girls have to tell me all about yourselves when you come on my show—so be ready for these dainty flowers on "The 'Power Hour!'" P.J. chuckles at her little joke.

"Now for the first runner-up. Ms. Davenport, may I have that envelope, please? I'm loving that new shade of lipstick—Destiny—was it named after you?"

Obviously, the S.N.A.P.S. lady must've shaken her head yes, because P.J. continues, "Y'all, run out and treat yourself to S.N.A.P.S. lipsticks—see, mine is still on, and I've been running my mouth *all* day—and you know I don't play! Oh, where was I?"

The audience chuckles again.

"That's right—I'd better open this envelope before one of those divettes backstage starts fainting. Our first runner-up is—the Cheetah Girls! Oh, they were too cute—growl power in the house tonight, y'all!"

We look at each other, and I see that Chanel has little tears in her eyes. Ms. Dorothea throws us all a look like, "Never let them see you sweat."

Running onto the stage, I feel so embarrassed. I *hate* losing, even though I know we didn't exactly *lose*. First runner-up isn't so bad, really—and a hundred dollars each is sure better than nothing, especially when you count in all the other free stuff we got—and our first time on the radio, too.

We stand next to P.J. Powers on the stage, and wait until the applause dies down. "I just wanna know, where did you girls get these cute outfits? Aren't they cute?" P.J. turns to the audience, and under the bright lights I can see she has too much makeup on. She is glowing like it's Halloween.

"Um, my mother is our designer," Galleria says proudly, and I can tell she is being more shy than usual.

"Yours even has a little tail on it—turn around so we can see that," P.J. says, pointing to me.

I'm so embarrassed, but I turn my booty to the audience—and they start laughing, then clapping. I feel like I just wanna do an abracadabra right on the spot and disappear!

"Now, people, I want y'all to know that *all* the divettes who performed in this competition are fierce—or they'd still be singing with their hairbrushes in the mirror! Am I right? That's right! So just because these girls didn't win first prize—a chance to compete in the finals— doesn't mean they aren't fierce. Honey, who knows? *They* could be the ones that go on and get the record deal!"

At least we still have a shot with Def Duck Records, I think gratefully. They're still willing to give us a chance. We are ushered off the stage, and wait with everyone else to hear who the winner is.

"Okay, y'all, I'm gonna get to it. Miss Lopez, would you hand me the envelope, please? You know I love your magazine. Where else can I read about 'How to Find a Man'? And Lord knows, I need one!"

Ms. Dorothea puts her arms around me and Galleria as we wait. "The winner is—Fakie Quakie!"

The two short girls let out a squeal like Miss Piggy, and jump up and down. I can't blame them. They must feel on top of the world.

"The battle is over!" P.J. says as the girls hit the stage. "Fakie Quakie, how do you two feel, now that you know you have a shot at appearing on MTV?"

"I'm not quaking anymore!" giggles the one who calls herself Quakie.

"Where are you girls from?"

"Mamaroneck," one of them says, and they both start giggling.

"Mamaroneck is in the house, y'all! The

Boogie-down Bronx can't get all the props—am I right?" P.J. squeals.

I can feel the stabbing pain in my chest again. Five hundred dollars—that is a dope prize, but it's not *first* prize, you know what I'm saying? Oh, well, at least my family wasn't here to see us come up short. Except now, I'm gonna have to find a way to tell them all about it. I am *not* lookin' forward to *that*.

After we change and head for the exit, Aqua says, "I'm not performing here anymore. This place is bad luck—with or without the Sandman."

"At least you girls won five hundred dollars—that's nothing to moan and groan about," Ms. Dorothea says sympathetically.

"We know, Mom," Galleria says, looking sad.

"*Madrina*, can we just leave?" Chanel asks, whining. "I don't want the people to see us crying."

"Now, if we don't find your mother outside, she will have a soap opera fit off the air, Chanel. You know that," Ms. Dorothea says, putting her arms around her. "If you girls don't want that five hundred dollars, I'll be very happy to take it and spend it for you."

What I'm thinking is, Ms. Dorothea deserves it more than we do. But I guess we don't have enough duckets in the bucket to be turning up our noses at any cash they want to give us.

"Are we gonna be on television?" Angie asks. "They were videotaping the show, weren't they?"

"The release didn't say the contest was going to air anywhere," Ms. Dorothea explains. "It's just a videotape for the production company's purposes—Looking Good Productions. They're the promoters of this competition, not MTV."

All of a sudden, I hear a squealing sound that's familiar. "Dorinda!" I look over and see—*Tiffany*! What is *she* doing here?

"Who's that?" Galleria asks curiously.

I freeze in my tracks, and don't say a word. Tiffany comes running over with this blond lady in a fur coat and a bald man wearing glasses. They must be her parents, I realize! Like a deer caught in the headlights of a car, I secretly pray I could do an *abracadabra*.

"You were dope!" Tiffany says, running up and giving me a hug.

I stand there, still frozen to the spot. "Hi," I

tell her—but my eyes are saying, "Why did you come here?"

"Hi, we're Tiffany's parents—I'm Brenda Twitty," the blond lady coos to me, "and this is my husband, Fred." Her hair is like a *bou bou fon fon*—it's piled really high and looks like it's hiding under a can of hairspray.

All of a sudden, you can feel the tension on the sidewalk. *All* of us seem really uncomfortable. Leave it to the twins to break the ice.

"Hi, I'm Aquanette Walker, and this is my twin sister, Anginette."

"I'm Tiffany—I'm Dorinda's sister," Tiffany says proudly. My crew just kinda looks at her, then at me. They've been over to my house, so they know Tiffany is not one of my foster sisters. Nobody says anything, though.

I feel so guilty and ashamed! Why did they have to come? We didn't even win the stupid competition!

"We've heard so much about you," Mrs. Twitty says warmly, putting a hand on my arm.

I guess I'm just staring at the ground, because Ms. Dorothea takes over, and chats with Tiffany and her parents about the show.

"You didn't tell us you invited your sister," Galleria says, like she's waiting for me to give her the lowdown.

"I didn't know she was coming," I say in a low voice.

Tiffany overhears us and pipes up, "Mrs. Bosco told me about the competition when I phoned—so I thought I would surprise Dorinda."

I can't believe Mrs. Bosco would do this to me! She *knows* how uncomfortable I am about people seeing me perform. I haven't even invited *her* yet!

"I hope you don't mind—I just wanted to surprise you," Tiffany says, her blue eyes twinkling. Then she turns to Chanel and says, "I wanna be a singer, too."

"Oh," Chanel says. "Do you sing?"

"Well, um, not like you all do—but I *want* to." The next thing I know, Chanel and Tiffany are deep in conversation—talking about which groups they like and who they think is cute! It's like they're already friends!

"Blanco from the Nastee Boys is really hot," Tiffany says, giggling.

"I have *un coco* on Krusher!" Chanel says,

breaking into a fit of hysterics. "I'm saving my first kiss for him!"

Galleria puts her arm around me and says, "Don't worry about it, Do'—just go with the flow."

I look at Galleria, and I just want to cry. She sees the tears in my eyes. I know I have a lot of explaining to do to my crew. But the main thing is, they've accepted Tiffany as my sister—just like that! Not one of them blinked twice at the fact that she was white.

What was I thinking? That my crew would be prejudiced? I see now how crazy that was— I mean, Galleria's half white herself, Ms. Dorothea married an Italian man, and Chuchie's got all kinds of mixed-up genes in her. They do look kind of surprised, of course— and I can tell I'm gonna have a lot of explaining to do later on. But the worst is over. Suddenly, I'm glad Tiffany showed up. It saved me having to break the news to my crew.

After what seems like forever, Tiffany and the Twittys say good night. "You wanna go to the park again?" Tiffany asks me, really sweetly.

"Okay," I say, and this time I really mean it.

"It's gonna be nice to have a real sister—someone who's got some of the same genes as me."

"And you're gonna tell me about genes, too—promise?" Tiffany begs.

I laugh, and put my arm around her shoulder. "I promise," I say. "I'll call you tomorrow, and we'll make a time to meet." We give each other a little kiss and a hug, and then I shake hands with her parents, promising to come over for dinner sometime.

When we get into Mr. Garibaldi's van, Galleria says, "Chanel is sneaky deaky, but Do' Re Mi, I've got to give it up to you—you sure do keep a lot of secrets!"

"I know," I admit. "But I only found out about Tiffany a week ago—and I didn't know how you'd all take it about her being white—and about me being half white."

Galleria smiles. "Just like me!" she says, giving me five. "Hey, it's a rainbow nation, *girlita!*"

All of a sudden, Galleria starts humming, "'Do' Re Mi on the Q.T./Do' Re Mi on the D.D.L./ That ain't swell./ Do' Re Mi on the Q.T./ Do' Re Mi on the D.D.L./ Why won't you tell?'"

"Hey! Now that's a song," coos Chanel.

"For once, Chuchie, you are right," Bubbles

says with a giggle. "Once more, I have come up with a master jammy whammy!"

I burst out laughing, 'cuz everything just seems so crazy! "Well—at least we got a song outta this situation!" I say. "And some money, too."

"And you got a new sister, too, looks like," Angie says.

"I like her," Chanel says, nodding slowly. "When you gonna bring her around sometime?"

"Pretty soon," I promise. "I thought you two might hit it off."

The car pulls into traffic. Aqua looks out the window and yells, "Good-bye Apollo—and the next time we come back, you're gonna have to *pay* us!"

I put my head on Chanel's shoulder and start us harmonizing on Galleria's new song: "'Do' Re Mi on the Q.T. Do' Re Mi on the D.D.L.'" I can't stop nodding to the beat. "It's definitely a whammy jammy," I tell Galleria.

The rest of the way home, I'm quiet. What a night! But I have to admit, the best part of it was Tiffany showing up like that—like she really cares about me.

I can't believe it—*I have a real sister!*

Do' Re Mi on the Q.T.

This is Galleria and this is Chanel
We are coming to you live
From Cheetah Girls Central
Where we process the data that matters
And even mad chatter
But today we're here to tell you
About our friend, Do' Re Mi
(That's Miss Dorinda to you)
Kats and Kittys, the drama
Has gotten so radikkio
Just when we thought we knew our crew
Bam! The scandal was told!

There's a new girl in town
That's Miss Dorinda to you,
She bounced into our lives
But now she's part of our crew

Do' Re Mi on the Q.T.
Do' Re Mi on the D.D.L.
(That ain't swell)
Do' Re Mi on the Q.T.

Do' Re Mi on the D.D.L.
(Why won't you tell?)

Dorinda's got a secret
And it's cutting off her flow
(Is that right, girlita?)
According to our sources,
She thought we didn't know
(Kats and Kittys, you'd better take notes)
Today for the first time (the very first time)
Do' Re Mi found out she's not alone
(What are you saying?)
She found out she got a sister
And it's making her moan and groan!

There's a new girl in town
That's Miss Dorinda to you,
She bounced into our lives
But now she's part of our crew

Do' Re Mi on the Q.T.
Do' Re Mi on the D.D.L.
(That ain't swell)
Do' Re Mi on the Q.T.
Do' Re Mi on the D.D.L.
(Why won't you tell?)

But we peeped you!
And now we beeped you!
So what you know about that, huh?

Let's tell Miss Dorinda
That she's got all the flavor
And when she keeps things to herself
It's Do' Re Mi that we savor
Don't turn quiet on us
Like you got nothing to say
We found out you got a sister
So why can't she come out and play?

Do' Re Mi on the Q.T.
Do' Re Mi on the D.D.L.
(That ain't swell)
Do' Re Mi on the Q.T.
Do' Re Mi on the D.D.L.
(Why won't you tell, tell, tell!)
We said Do' Re Mi's on the Q.T.
(That's the sneak tip)
Do' Re Mi on the D.D.L.
(That's the down, down low)
Do' Re Mi on the Q.T.
Do' Re Mi on the D.D.L.

Do' Re Mi on the Q.T.
Who you trying to be?
Do' Re Mi on the D.D.L.
That's right, you know that's fowl
like a nearsighted owl
Do' Re Mi on the Q.T.
Why you got secrets
that make us growl?
Do' Re Mi on the D.D.L.
(Is that really true her sister is—Ahhhh!
Yes, mamacita . . .)

(Fade with growl sounds)

The Cheetah Girls Glossary

Ad-lipping: Talking nonsense. Blabbing with
an attitude.

Amped: Excited. As in, "What are you so
amped about?"

Angle for a dangle: Cheesing or manipulating
a situation so you can get a chomp on the
carrot dangling in your face. Kinda like
angling for an "op," but more cheesing is
involved.

Audi 5000: Gone like the Road Runner. To do a
fast getaway.

Beaucoup swelly: Supa cool.

Beef jerky: Static. When you have a beef with
someone.

Big Willy: Someone who is really important.
Something that is really dope.

Blab your trap: Talk too much.

Blow up: Become really really successful.

Bozo: A boy who thinks he's all that but he isn't.

Coming out of the box: All of a sudden. Out of
the blue but not true blue—not for real.

D.D.L.: On the down, down low. For example: you just got your report card and you got a C in biology. When you get home, you run to your room and stay on the D.D.L. from your mom until dinnertime.

Enuf with the powder puff: Dress rehearsal is over. It's show time, baby.

Emphatically: On the serious tip.

Feels like a "Magilla Gorilla": Feels too heavy.

Fib-eronis: Teeny weeny fibs. Purple lies and alibis!

Flex and floss: Do your thing. Make things happen faster than Minute Rice.

Hoax-arama: Something that isn't true.

Hunky chunky: Cool, fine, as in: "Everything is fine" (even if it isn't).

Jammy whammy: A dope song. As in, "That's a master jammy whammy!"

Joint: Supa chili. As in, "That song is the joint."

Jumpstreet: The place where you get to the point, as in, "You shoulda just asked me that from jumpstreet."

Muslin: Plain white fabric used for draping and making a pattern for clothes.

Piggly-wiggly giggle: An oinky-sounding laugh.

Posse: Crew. The peeps you hang with.

Put in check: Straightening out someone who is dissing you. Letting them know, it's not like that, okay?

Q.T.: On the hush, hush, sneak, sneaky or the quick tip.

Radikkio: Ridiculous. As in, "Don't be radikkio!"

Rigor mortis: Temporary stiffening of muscles in a corpse.

Spastic-on-the-elastic tip: Someone who doesn't know how to go with the flow.

The big bulb from above: The mysterious source of all Big Willy ideas.

The spookies: The "willies."

Thinking without blinking: When you really know something is true.

To hype up: Support. Represent to the max.

Toodles: Bye. See you later.

Toodly: Fine, okay. Like when someone asks you, 'How are you?' You respond, "I'm toodly."

Twizzling: Twisting something into pretzel shapes or just messing around with it.

ABOUT THE AUTHOR

Deborah Gregory earned her growl power as a diva-about-town contributing writer for ESSENCE, VIBE, and MORE magazines. She has showed her spots on several talk shows, including OPRAH, RICKI LAKE, and MAURY POVICH. She lives in New York City with her pooch, Cappuccino, who is featured as the Cheetah Girls' mascot, Toto.

 JUMP AT THE SUN

the Cheetah girls

THE CHEETAHS ARE ROCKIN' & HOLLYWOOD IS KNOCKIN'!!

Aquanette & Anginette are in Houston visiting their mom when— lo and behold— they get a phone call that can change the Cheetahs' lives forever!

Cheetah Girls #8: Growl Power

AVAILABLE AUGUST 2000

the Cheetah girls

Catch up with the Girls

#1 Wishing on a Star
0-7868-1384-9

#2 Shop in the Name of Love
0-7868-1385-7

#3 Who's 'Bout to Bounce?
0-7868-1386-5

#4 Hey, Ho, Hollywood!
0-7868-1387-3

#5 Woof, There It Is
0-7868-1424-1

#6 It's Raining Benjamins
0-7868-1425-X

They're Cheetah-licious!

Hey, Girlfriend!

Would you like to be a member of our club?

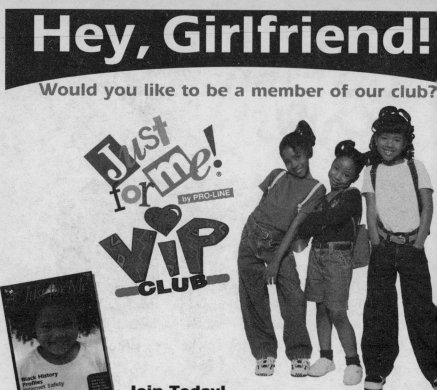

Just for me!® by PRO-LINE

VIP CLUB

Black History
Profiles
Internet Safety
VIP Parties

Join Today!

Become a Just for Me VIP Member and get the official club membership kit today!
The membership kit includes a Just for Me VIP Club: Membership Card, Newsletter, Do Not Disturb Door Hanger, Passport to Fun, Scrungies, Bookmark, Coupons, ID Fingerprint Card, and Membership Flyer. In addition, you will receive a birthday card, a birthday surprise, and bimonthly newsletters.

Official Enrollment Form: Make sure you fill this form out completely. Print clearly. We cannot be responsible for lost, late, misdirected, or illegible mail. Enclose $9.95 plus one Just for Me proof of purchase (front panel), for membership in the JFM VIP Club, or $19.95 with no proof of purchase. Make check or money order (no cash) payable to: Just for Me VIP Club c/o Pro-Line Corp., P.O. Box 222057, Dallas, Texas 75222-9831

Name: _____ Date of Birth: _____

Address: _____

City: _____ State: _____ ZIP: _____

Day Phone: _____ Evening Phone: _____

Parent signature: _____

Mail membership forms to: Pro-Line Corporation   Attn: JFM VIP Club Membership   P.O. Box 222057   Dallas, TX 75222-9831

The Pro-Line Company is not affiliated with The Walt Disney Company